ORBU!

In every direction that they Read, they found people. People? They were flesh and blood and human bodies moving toward them, breathing, hearts beating—but there seemed to be no minds within them. All Adepts braced to use their powers. But so many? It was hopeless. It seemed like an army of the dead!

"Orbu!" gasped Dirdra.

"They're mindless—but they *are* alive!" said Melissa, and as one of them raised a spear as if to heave it at her she neatly stopped the creature's heart. It dropped, truly dead.

Torio and Zanos drew their swords, lopping off heads as wave after wave of mindless beings surged through the woods, enveloping the five companions in their sheer numbers. Torio could not count how many he killed, but the things seemed more agitated, more determined. Then, daring to focus beyond his immediate vicinity, Torio realized—"Maldek's run out of them! These are the last!" But the latecomers were sturdier. . . .

*Sorcerers
of the
Frozen Isles*
A Tale of the Savage Empire

by Jean Lorrah

Ⓢ
A SIGNET BOOK
NEW AMERICAN LIBRARY

NAL BOOKS ARE AVAILABLE AT QUANTITY DISCOUNTS WHEN
USED TO PROMOTE PRODUCTS OR SERVICES. FOR INFORMA-
TION PLEASE WRITE TO PREMIUM MARKETING DIVISION, NEW
AMERICAN LIBRARY, 1633 BROADWAY, NEW YORK, NEW YORK
10019.

SIGNET, SIGNET CLASSIC, MENTOR, PLUME, MERIDIAN AND NAL BOOKS
are published by New American Library,
1633 Broadway, New York, New York 10019

First Printing, May, 1986

1 2 3 4 5 6 7 8 9

PRINTED IN THE UNITED STATES OF AMERICA

Foreword

The entire *Savage Empire* series is dedicated to the person who got me into professional sf writing and then encouraged me to start my own series:

Jacqueline Lichtenberg

I would also like to thank the many readers who have sent comments about the first four books in the series: I hope you enjoy this fifth book in the *Savage Empire* universe.

If there are readers who would like to comment on this book, my publisher will forward letters to me. If you prefer, you may write to me directly at Box 625, Murray, KY 42071. If your letter requires an answer, please enclose a stamped self-addressed envelope.

All comments are welcome. I came to professional writing through fan writing and publishing, where there is close and constant communication between writers and readers. Thus I shall always be grateful for the existence of sf fandom, which has provided me with many exciting experiences, and through which I have met so many wonderful people.

Jean Lorrah
Murray, Kentucky

Chapter One

S pring sunshine warmed the air. Birds sang, butterflies danced among the flowers, and Torio, Lord Reader of the newly expanded Savage Empire, brooded as he rode beside Lord Wulfston. They were on their way to Zendi, temporary capital of their strange alliance and home to Lenardo and Aradia, unofficial leaders of that alliance.

But no place here is my *home,* Torio thought.

He had grown up in the Academy at Adigia, a powerful young Reader expecting to spend his life using his powers to benefit citizens of the Aventine Empire. Now there was no more Aventine Empire.

And it's my fault.

No, it wasn't his doing alone, but he had been a major factor in the force which had quite literally tumbled an empire, creating an earthquake that caused the earth to open and swallow up its capital city. Now they had a huge area to try to govern—a country full of hostile people whose lives had just been devastated.

They had left the worst of it to Lenardo and Aradia after the fall of Tiberium, and Wulfston had returned to his own lands, acquired only the year before. Even though the new Lord of the Land had made life much better for his people in his short reign, there was still a danger that their trust in him could not survive a long absence.

So Wulfston had gone home to secure his seaside kingdom—and Lenardo had urged Torio to continue to work with the Adept. "Wulfston knows how to teach people to obey him," his teacher had said, "and still to love him. That is an ability you must have before you can rule your own land."

Ruling a land—it was not what Readers were born to in the Aventine Empire. But Lenardo insisted that Torio's insecurity stemmed from youth. He had been only eighteen when his teacher told him that, and a Magister Reader—or at least Lenardo and Master Clement insisted he was.

Torio had never taken the formal tests of his powers, but if there was one thing he *was* secure about, it was that he would have passed the most stringent tests the Council of Masters might have devised. His Reading was the one stable element in his life—it had to be, for he had been born blind. Without his Reading ability, he would have spent his life as a helpless liability to the family he had been born into. As it was, he perceived the world far better than any sighted nonReader.

But what was he supposed to do with those powers now? All the rules had changed. Grown up in the communal life of the Academy, barred by law from owning property or holding public office, now Torio had treasures beyond imagination, and lands held in his name that he would rule one day. Expecting to be sworn to celibacy once he entered the top ranks of Readers, now he was told he could marry if he so desired, without risking the loss of his powers.

He often thought about that possibility . . . about Melissa. When his thoughts turned to her, they lightened—one good thing about this journey to Zendi was that he would get to see Melissa again! In the past year he had seen her only three times in person, although as Readers they had frequent mental contact.

In the midst of his pleasant reverie, the sunny day suddenly plunged into blackness. Torio heard a rumbling, felt the jostling of a crowd. He was being pulled along, trying to escape—

The noise grew louder, nearer, more terrifying, bearing down as people shouted incoherent warnings—

Screams!

The tug at him was suddenly gone—he was alone in a crowd, lost, panicked, as something rumbled and rolled over human flesh, crushing bones, the smell of blood and fear sweat rising—

"Torio! Torio—what's the matter with you?"

At Wulfston's voice, Torio suddenly realized that he was Reading something actually happening not far away. He focused his powers, and found—

"Wulfston—a man's being crushed to death! We've got to help him!"

"Where?" was Wulfston's only question. They were still in the Lord Adept's lands—he would never withhold his powers when one of his people needed him.

"This way!" answered Torio, and set off at a gallop, first along the road, then off it toward a stone quarry scarring the side of the range of hills that would intersect the road in a few more miles.

Wulfston did not need to be told what had happened—when they reached the scene, everything was instantly obvious.

These people were a family, earning their living by cutting rock from the hillside for building in Wulfston's lands or in Zendi. The quarry was new, for the latest Lords of the Land had begun a spate of building such as had not been seen in most people's lifetimes.

Beneath the steep walls created by their work, they had been easing a huge block of granite down an earthen ramp, controlling it with block and tackle, when the ropes had given way. The stone had trapped the legs of a young man in his twenties, who now lay helpless while the others tried to remove the rock or dig him out from under it. Shock had left him unconscious, so Torio no longer had to endure his pain as he Read beneath the rock.

"Wulfston, his left leg is almost torn off—he's bleeding to death. They'll never get him out alive!"

Indeed, the old man and two strong young men flinging their picks at the ground were making little progress—the pathway down which they slid the quarried stones had been worn to the living, unyielding rock.

Another young man, shivering even though his skin was covered with sweat, swore steadily as he tried to make his shaking hands ravel together the broken ropes to haul the stone off . . . his brother, Torio Read.

Two women, the younger one obviously pregnant, knelt beside the pinned man, wiping his face—but there was nothing they could do. His life was slipping away as his mother and his wife watched.

Another woman grabbed a pick and added her unskilled efforts to the task as Wulfston and Torio rode up. Down the slope, near the house, four children watched with huge eyes, not understanding what was happening, but too frightened to cry.

The three women looked up as the riders approached, but the men would not leave off their efforts.

"Me lord!" cried the older woman. "Oh, me lord—please help my boy! I'll do anything—"

These people might never have seen Wulfston before, or perhaps have glimpsed him only at a distance at some ceremonial or other, but they knew the Lord of the Land at once. He was the only black man Torio knew of north of what had been the empire's border.

As he and Torio got down from their horses, Wulfston hushed the mother and the rest of the family, saying, "We'll help. Torio—is he alive?"

Gray with shock, the young man lay so still that it was impossible to tell by looking at him, but Torio Read him. "Yes, but he won't be for long. If he's not out from under there in minutes—"

"Oh, Bevan!" groaned the young man's wife.

"Then there's no choice but to move the rock," said Wulfston. "You men—get over on the other side and haul on the ropes. I'm going to use your strength as well as mine. When I tell you, tilt the block toward you."

Torio knew moving that huge block of granite by Adept power alone—working directly against gravity—would tax Wulfston's strength close to its limit. He almost started to tell the Lord Adept not to allow himself to become so vulnerable—but he shook off that thought. There was no question but that Bevan's life had to be saved! How could such a selfish idea even cross his mind?

He had no time to examine where a thought so unlike his normal Reader's instinct had come from, for Wulfston was bracing to use his powers, becoming completely unReadable as the strong quarrymen took their places on the opposite side of the rock, tightening the ropes.

Torio knelt beside the pinned man, waiting for the moment when the rock shivered, lifted—

"Higher!" he exclaimed, securing his grip under the young man's shoulders.

Trembling, the block of stone crept upward another handspan—and Torio hauled Bevan out from under just before it dropped again with a thunderous "whump!"

Torio grasped the young man's leg, where bright arterial blood pumped out, squeezing to keep the last of his life from spilling onto the rocky ground. "Wulfston!"

The Adept had sunk to his knees in recovery from his effort to lift the rock. He looked blankly toward Torio for a moment, then pulled himself away from the desire to collapse and came to Torio's side. "Straighten his leg," he instructed Torio. "Unite the blood vessels."

Torio did as he was told, feeling Wulfston go unReadable again. Torio Read carefully, holding the major vessels while Wulfston concentrated, and they healed together, normal blood flow resuming. Only then did he shove together the splintered bone ends, watching them knit miraculously together into a tenuous bond. Then, with Bevan's wife and mother tenderly cleansing the wounds, the torn muscles were healed, but—

"The nerves, Wulfston."

"I can't," the Adept said wearily. "Make certain all will stay alive for now—the rest will have to be healed later."

The audience of quarrymen and their families stared as Bevan's torn skin was carefully drawn back over his leg. Large chunks were missing, but the leg was saved, along with his life.

Finally, the heat of Adept healing spread beneath Torio's hands, killing any infection that had been introduced, and continuing the healing as the young man slept. Torio had seen it a hundred times, but every time it was a new miracle: Wulfston had set in motion the healing powers of Bevan's own body, which he could not activate on his own. He would continue to sleep and heal even after Wulfston left him, probably for more than a day before he woke with his pain gone and his leg well on the way to being whole again.

Wulfston had sat down, tailor-fashion, to concentrate on the healing. Now he remained still, withdrawn—Torio wondered if he would fall asleep right there. His tiredness was now completely Readable.

But after a few moments he looked up, blinking. "Your son will heal," he told the anxious parents. "Carry him to your house, and let him sleep until he wakens naturally. Then feed him—he will need a great deal of food to restore his strength.

Don't let him try to walk. His leg is alive, but he will not be able to feel it until the nerves are healed. When I return from Zendi, you must bring him to my castle. There Torio and I will finish the healing."

Bevan's father and his brothers carried him carefully down to the house, his mother hurrying ahead to prepare his bed.

"Oh, my lord!" Bevan's wife knelt beside Wulfston, sobbing. "I thought sure he was dead, my lord! How can we ever repay you?"

"No need," Wulfston replied. "It is my duty to keep my people healthy—I'm just glad I was nearby. However, if you can provide me with something to eat—?"

"Wulfston!" Torio warned suddenly. "Someone's coming!" And to the woman he ordered, "Run! Get into the house!"

As Bevan's wife fled clumsily down the path, around the side of the hill came armed riders in the ragtag garb of hill bandits. They ignored the fleeing woman, charging directly for Wulfston and Torio.

There were a dozen men, enough to make an Adept waste his powers until he made himself helpless—provided they knew exactly how to trick him into doing so.

And it appeared that they knew what they were doing, for despite his tiredness after moving the quarried stone, Wulfston sent a sheet of flame roaring up out of the ground before their horses. The animals screamed and reared, but in moments the riders had them under control and were charging once more toward the two men, cutting off their chance of escape down the path.

Wulfston did not kill indiscriminately; Torio knew he meant to frighten the attackers off, but he hadn't succeeded.

"Wulfston—save your strength!" said Torio, grasping the Adept by the arm and hauling him behind the rock as the bandits drew close enough to shoot arrows from short bows. They clattered off the rock, but the men kept coming, those without bows now drawing throwing knives.

And below them on the slope, four other bandits rode toward the quarriers' house with torches. In moments the thatch roof was ablaze.

From their position, Wulfston could see what was happening below. Instantly, his responsibility for his people asserted itself, and he concentrated on putting out the blaze—again working against nature, for once that dry straw had begun to flame, it would have gone up instantly without Adept powers to stem it.

"Wulfston, they're dividing your attention!" Torio warned. "Put those men down there to sleep!"

That the Adept had the power to do, but Torio could Read him clutching the granite block for support, and feared that the dozen men drawing in for the kill might be too many for Wulfston to handle. The young Reader drew his sword, prepared to defend Wulfston and himself to the extent of his strength and skill.

The huge stone blocked the path, so that the attackers could get through only on one side. Three men jumped off their horses and started around. The first one ran straight into Torio's sword, for the Reader could tell every move he planned and be ready for him.

At their companion's death cry, the other two charged forward together.

Torio was a skilled swordsman—and, thank the gods, these two were not. He used the advantage of his sightless eyes, letting them drift unfocused, unnerving his opponents as they realized they were battling a blind swordsman.

But even as Torio held the two at bay, the nine other bandits leaped from their horses and began to climb over the granite block, aided by the ropes still slung around it.

"Wulfston—they're climbing over the stone! Retreat!"

The Adept, though, took another action. The ropes around the mighty stone blazed into flame, and the bandits dropped off, yowling, sucking at burned hands.

Starting fires, Torio knew, was one of the easiest of Adept skills, taking very little power. As the flame sizzled around the ropes to where he fought with the two bandits, one of them started at the noise, allowing Torio to get in under his guard and skewer him.

As a Reader, Torio had to deal swift death or suffer with his victim. He shoved his keen-edged sword upward to pierce the man's heart.

The other man's fear sweat was a stench in Torio's nostrils, but in terror he slashed at the Reader, forgetting what little style he had had as he drove the younger man back with the sheer power of panic.

Torio evaded his blows, letting him waste the charge of adrenaline, waiting for an opening—

But Wulfston did not wait. Seeing Torio apparently being beaten back, he stopped the man's heart, and the bandit dropped at Torio's feet.

Just as Torio looked toward Wulfston, though, the fire consuming the thick ropes around the huge rock reached the underside—and as their support collapsed to ashes the stone shifted and slid.

Wulfston grasped the moment. Working with the already-moving stone, he sent it skidding sideways, right toward the bandits on the pathway, crushing them to death against the side of the quarry.

Torio gasped with their death agony, but in moments it was over, and he turned to Wulfston just as—

Above them, on the edge of the quarry, more bandits appeared. Minor Adepts, they joined hands and concentrated together—just as they must have done to crush Bevan under that rock! It was all a trap—a ruse to draw Wulfston here and use up his powers so that he was helpless before their minor abilities.

A sheet of flame rose out of the pathway. Wulfston swore as he and Torio ducked away from it, the Adept stumbling with weariness.

"Why didn't you Read them?" Wulfston demanded.

"They were braced to use their powers," Torio explained. "With everything else going on—"

But even as he spoke, the gang at the top of the quarry were focusing on him.

He felt his heart falter. Pain clutched at his chest as he gasped, "Wulfston, they're—"

Wulfston saw at once that the young Reader was in pain, and Torio felt Adept power set his heart back into a normal pattern. But how much strength could Wulfston have left?

As he panted for breath, Torio felt a peculiar sick knowledge that he had not Read the whole story. The minor Adepts were retreating, and from behind them—

"Wulfston! There are other men up there!"

His warning came too late. New attackers suddenly dropped out of the sky.

They leaped from the top of the quarry—stronger Adepts, able to protect themselves from injury in the fall—and they were armed.

Knives and swords flashed—each man was a living weapon, a sword in one hand, a knife in the other, blades on their feet, on their elbows, leaping toward Wulfston, toward Torio.

Death came slashing through the air, the attackers using gravity, only guiding their fall to be certain to land on their victims.

It took a mere split-second, too short a time for Wulfston and Torio to run, with no shelter closer than the house far down the pathway.

Torio Read death upon him, three men falling toward him, one slashing for his head even as the young Reader lifted his sword and prepared to take at least one of them with him—

Flame!

Screams!

In midair, the falling men burst into flame!

Their kicking and writhing changed their course —the one attempting to decapitate Torio bounced off the quarry wall, sword clattering on the rocks as he landed uncontrolled, the pain of broken legs unfelt in the agony of burning flesh.

The seven who had dropped on them burned

and screamed—five able to stand, dancing and shrieking as the fire ate from the outside in.

"Wulfston!" Torio screamed in the men's agony. "Kill them! *Kill them!*" His own flesh seemed to sear and flake off as theirs did, so caught was he in their death throes.

Instead, a sheet of flame engulfed the other attackers watching from the quarry rim, sending them screaming and writhing and dancing the hideous dance of death as their flesh cooked off their bones, taking their hearts and brains last.

Only as the last man died could Torio stop Reading, cutting off the pain but leaving him blind, closed in on himself, sweating and shaking—and then vomiting as the stench of burnt flesh assaulted him anew.

Finally, he had to Read again. Still trembling, he Read slowly outward, finding only corpses.

They were all dead. There was no more pain.

Wulfston, as open to being Read as a nonAdept, was fighting not to pass out.

But he *was* awake, and that meant—

"How much strength would it have taken to stop their hearts?" Torio demanded. "Why did you let them die so horribly?"

Wulfston turned weary eyes to Torio. "Are there any more?"

Torio Read. No new attackers lurked anywhere around, nor was anyone fleeing. All were dead—even the ones down by the house, he Read sickly. Wulfston hadn't chanced just putting them to sleep, lest they waken after he had exhausted his powers. "No. You killed them all," he said flatly.

"Are you hurt?" asked the Lord Adept.

"No, but—"

"But you might have required healing," explained Wulfston.

Torio knew, intellectually, why the Adept was trained to save the last of his strength in a situation such as they had just gone through—a last-resort means of escape or healing.

But his heart still protested the agony Wulfston had allowed.

"Torio, can you get me to the stonecutter's cottage?" Wulfston asked.

"Yes, if you can walk. Lean on me."

The needs of a Lord Adept who had expended his powers for them was something the stonecutter's family understood—and Torio was glad to see that it was no hardship for them to meet even the appetite of a Lord Adept. They were welcomed joyfully into the house, where the main room served as kitchen, dining hall, and family gathering place. There was meat aplenty, just what an Adept required to restore energy quickly after using his powers.

At the gratitude of the innocent people the bandits had used so cruelly, Torio accepted that they had done what they had to—Reader and Adept working together, to protect those without their powers. Feeling better by the moment, he ate tasty brown bread with butter, the ubiquitous cooked vegetables, fresh berries, and a rich tart served with cream—a meal designed to give strength to men who worked the quarry.

He had to explain that Readers did not eat meat, and discovered that everyone had thought him an apprentice Adept, since Readers were still scarce in this part of the savage lands.

Bevan's family put Wulfston to bed in the loft

where the married couples slept, and were astonished to find that Torio was wide awake—and full
of questions about where their attackers had come
from. If only they had left one of them alive!

"I dinna understand," said Morgone, the old
stonecutter who headed the family. "We've had
naught o' trouble wi' bandits. People herebouts,
they like what Lord Wulfston's done. We got homes,
food—who needs turn bandit?"

"I don't know," Torio told him, "but we're going
to find out."

Although he had explained that Reading took
no physical energy, Torio did accept a bed and
went up to it early, for he had messages to deliver.

To cover the distances he must now Read, Torio
had to leave his body. Had his training at the
Academy proceeded normally, at his age he would
be undertaking such an exercise occasionally, under the guidance of a teacher. The events of the
past two years, however, had required him to Read
over distances so often that leaving his body had
become commonplace.

He smoothed the bed and lay down carefully,
positioned so that his circulation could not be cut
off while his body was unoccupied. Then he allowed his "self" to drift upward.

Immediately, his Reading took on a clarity possible only when the flesh was left behind. No longer
did he have to visualize the world deliberately; it
was all there, without effort and without restriction.

He Read outward from the stonecutter's cottage, searching for signs of further danger. A few
miles down the road there was an inn, where local
farmers sometimes stopped for a cup of ale at this
time of day. That's all they were—farmers, the

innkeeper, and his wife and three daughters, one
of them flirting with a local farm lad.

But there were no strangers, no travelers, and
no one with a worry in his head except the boy
wondering if the girl he favored cared for him, or
whether she acted this way with other customers.

Ignoring the inn, Torio scanned the fields, empty
or emptying. Nothing more sinister there than
rabbits and field mice. Nor did the woodlands
harbor people, except for a woodcutter who lived
there and a patrol of Wulfston's foresters out to
see that no one took deer out of season.

Then where had their attackers come from?

As Morgone said, there was no widespread dis-
satisfaction among Wulfston's people. Only the
bandits who preyed on travelers were unhappy
that the new Lord of the Land did not take the
attitude of Drakonius, who had ignored them as
long as they did not interfere with his plans for
conquest.

Wulfston's first impulse had been to give the
bandits fair warning to mend their ways—and then
wipe out the ones who refused to turn to farming,
hunting, woodcutting, or other honest occupation.
However, too many outlaws were distrustful, having suffered many years of Drakonius' unpredict-
ability. Furthermore, they considered this new lord,
with his preference for alliance over conquest, to
be dangerously weak—easy prey for the next
Drakonius.

Over the nearly two years of Wulfston's reign,
though, he had made the main roads safe. Many
outlaws had decided that the risks of being caught
now that there were Readers in the land out-
weighed the risks of pledging loyalty to the new

lord. The rest moved northward, out of the area
ruled by the alliance of Adepts and Readers who
called their union the Savage Empire.

It was not Torio who had persuaded Wulfston
not to track down all the outlaws and summarily
execute them. It was Jareth, his chief adviser from
among his newly inherited people, who had pointed
out that under Drakonius' rule many, many people had been so plundered as to be left with little
choice except to prey on others to survive. While
the majority had returned gratefully to honest
work at Wulfston's invitation, there were enough
suspicious ones that nearly everyone had kin or
friend still outlaw. Wholesale slaughter of the hill
bandits might well have turned hesitantly loyal
followers against Wulfston once again.

Torio had agreed with Jareth, although for a
Reader's reasons: enduring the pain and death of
other people turned any Reader against violence
as a solution to violence.

After today's experience, though, he wondered
if he could have been wrong. Might there have
been less suffering in the long run had the bandits
been permanently eliminated? They had obviously
taken Wulfston's decision as a sign of weakness.
How many other bands of minor Adepts were
there? What would they learn from what had happened today?

At least they would be easier to find in the
future. This trip to Zendi was to meet with some
of the Readers who walked the Path of the Dark
Moon—those who had not the strength or skill to
attain the rank of Magister or Master, but whose
numbers had formerly made them the eyes and
ears of an empire. Wulfston intended to offer

them his protection and a comfortable living in exchange for their forming such a network in his land.

Today, though, there was only Torio. Having determined that there were no other bandits hiding within a day's ride in Wulfston's lands, he Read along the little-used trail to the north, out beyond the border.

There, in the rough terrain where the chain of hills became the foothills of mighty mountains, Torio found a camp. There must have been two hundred people, men, women, and children living in makeshift shelters, tents, covered wagons, and pine-branch lean-tos. It was a sort of semipermanent community which could easily pack up and move—as they seemed to be preparing to do soon.

The camp buzzed with excitement and expectation. Torio had no trouble Reading what was on every mind: within the next few days their leaders would return to tell them they had killed the upstart Wulfston, and they would move in and take over his lands, turning them into an outlaw kingdom where they could live at ease, plundering the foolish ones who still toiled in the fields.

No one here knew that their leaders, those with some Adept powers, lay dead in the quarry far inside Wulfston's lands. Not one had escaped to tell the tale.

Torio knew that, leaderless, they would probably break up again into small outlaw bands ... until they could coerce some other minor Adepts to try once more to unite against one lone Lord Adept. At least that was what he told Lenardo when he contacted him in Zendi a few minutes later.

He let Lenardo Read the day's experience directly from his mind, and then waited for his mentor's comments.

//You've done very well, Torio,// Lenardo told him. //Not long ago you would have come to me immediately, instead of searching for the outlaw camp with your own powers.//

//But what should we do about them?// Torio asked.

Lenardo had left his wife and daughter to entertain Lilith and her son Ivorn, who had just arrived. Now he was in his study, at the table which he and Aradia used for a desk. He selected a map. //The camp is not in our territory. I do not know whether one of the Lords Adept to the north of us considers that area his, or whether everyone leaves that terrain to bandits and wanderers. I don't think that camp will break up for a few days—they have no way of knowing what happened to their attack force until they send someone to investigate. You found no sign of Readers among them? Somehow they found out that Wulfston would be traveling without a retinue.//

//No Readers,// Torio told him with total certainly. //Spies in Zendi would have heard we were expected, and then it would have been easy enough for just one person to watch Wulfston's castle to see whether people gathered to form a retinue. And he's known for avoiding unnecessary ceremony. Besides, I should think that since it's an alliance of Readers with Adepts that has made their life difficult as bandits, they'd be even more distrustful of Readers than most savages.//

Lenardo smiled. //Who are the savages, Torio? Anybody who isn't us?// But he obviously didn't expect an answer. //Get some rest. I'll Read the outlaw camp in the morning, to make sure they're not planning to move before we can decide what to do about them.//

//All right, as soon as I've reported to Rolf what happened today—Wulfston's household must think we're with you by now, unless the watchers have reported otherwise. And if they have, they'll be worried about us.//

//Good thinking—always be considerate of those who depend on you.//

So Torio withdrew—and then sought the opposite direction, back to the castle where he and Wulfston had begun their journey. It was still early evening; Rolf was just finishing a consulation with local farmers concerning the amount of rain needed in the next week.

Rolf, like Torio, had been born blind, but with a single Adept power: control of weather. Then last summer, with the help of Torio and Melissa, he had learned to Read. Now, although he would never have Torio's abilities, he no longer used a stick to find his way around, nor required anyone to guide him. Even with only limited Reading power, he was happy with his newfound independence.

At the moment, he was the only Reader at Wulfston's castle. He could never have Read to the stonecutter's cottage where Torio was, but a stronger Reader could always contact a weaker one. When Torio touched Rolf's mind, the other boy quickly responded, //Have you reached Zendi already?//

//No, but both Wulfston and I are unhurt.//

Only after that reassurance did he explain what had happened.

//How could anyone *want* to attack you and Lord Wulfston?// Rolf asked in genuine bewilderment. //Lord Torio, you and Wulfston must not travel without a retinue again.//

//We'll worry about that some other time. What you must do now is watch for spies around the castle. *Somebody* knew when Wulfston would be traveling, and that he and I would be alone. That person probably left the area when we did—but be alert for other strangers, Rolf. If one band of malcontents could hatch such a plot, it's always possible there could be others.//

//Yes, my lord,// Rolf told him, and Torio knew security would be redoubled. So when he broke contact and returned to his body, he was able to relax in the knowledge that he had done everything he had to, and fall asleep—only to toss and turn with nightmares that disappeared when he woke, shaking, with a haunting sense of guilt.

When Wulfston and Torio reached Zendi the next day, everyone in their circle already knew what had happened, and agreed that something had to be done about the outlaw band. "If nothing else," said Aradia, "we must make an example of them, so that no one else decides we are easy prey."

She hugged her brother, a striking visual contrast between the small, pale woman with hair so light a blond it looked white in some lights, and the tall black man who called her sister. Wulfston at least looked strong. Aradia's apparent frailty belied the incredible Adept powers at her com-

mand, for she was in the prime of her powers
and still growing—as was Lenardo.

Wulfston had been adopted by Aradia's father
when his Adept powers manifested in early childhood. The two children had somehow grown up
best of friends, closer than many siblings by blood.
There were still times when Wulfston knew better than Lenardo how to cope with Aradia's
willfulness.

The group of people who together ruled the
Savage Empire had grown to include Lenardo,
Aradia, Wulfston, Torio, Melissa, Lilith, Ivorn,
and Master Clement, who had been teacher to
both Lenardo and Torio. Melissa was not there
when they arrived; she was at the hospital set up
here in Zendi so that the most seriously ill or
injured need not be taken all the way to Gaeta for
expert care. A Reader grown up in an Academy,
like Torio, she had already been a skilled healer
when she learned to use Adept powers, and now
her ability to cure was almost miraculous.

Torio went to his room and unpacked clean
clothes, eager for the luxury of a genuine bath.
At Wulfston's castle he could have a shower, the
water warmed by the sun on the rooftop cistern,
or in winter a hot bath with the water hauled by
servants to his room. But Zendi, which had once
been an Aventine city, had real plumbing—and it
was put to full use in the luxurious bathhouse.

Decius, a young Reader who had come here
with Master Clement, joined him, walking easily
on his wooden leg. "Zanos says the Master Sorcerers of Madura might be able to grow me a new
leg," he announced as he removed his peg before
sliding into the water.

"What?" Torio asked in confusion. He recalled Zanos, the huge red-haired gladiator who had turned out to have minor Adept powers. He had seduced a female Reader—Torio couldn't remember her name. The two had escaped the Aventine Empire in the chaos of the short war last summer, and ingratiated themselves with Lilith by keeping another band of outlaws from taking over her castle and stealing her treasures while she was away.

"He's been asking everybody about Madura," Decius explained in typical adolescent carelessness for logical connections. "That's where he was born, and kidnapped and brought to Tiberium to be a gladiator. I mean, he was captured as a little boy, and then when he grew up—"

"I understand, Decius," said Torio, luxuriating in water deep enough to swim in. "What's this about Master Sorcerers?"

"I guess that's what they call Adepts there— but they're Readers, too, and they can do lots more than *our* Adepts. At least, that's what the legends say. Some sailors said—"

"Sailors' tales, Decius? Aren't you a good enough Reader to tell they make most of their adventures up?"

"Well, other people say it, too. They say they can make cut-off limbs grow back—they could probably fix your eyes, too."

"I get along just fine without them," Torio reminded him.

"Well . . . they say they have the power to fly. And do real magic, like turning men into monkeys. And—they even say they can bring the dead back to life!"

Torio laughed, and lunged for Decius, ducking him. The younger boy retaliated, pulling Torio under, then waiting to splash water in his face when he emerged snorting.

But Torio was bigger and stronger, and the better Reader. Decius could not shield his thoughts as well, so Torio knew which move he would make next, and captured the wriggling boy to duck him again.

When Decius shot out of the depths, blowing water out of his mouth, Torio caught him and pinned him against the pool wall for a moment. "Decius, stories like that are fun to tell around the fire in the evening, but you *know* they are misunderstandings, if they're not totally imaginary. Did you counter the sailors by telling them you have a friend who was raised from the dead?"

"Well, uh—" Torio Read that the boy had had to work very hard not to yield to that temptation.

"You see? You know I wasn't dead—just some nonReaders *thought* I was, so when I turned up alive they thought the savage healers had brought me back. That's how accurate you can expect those stories the sailors told you to be. Flying, indeed!"

"Why not, if the Adept is powerful enough?" Decius demanded stubbornly.

"How long can *any* Adept work directly against nature? Or did your sailors claim that these sorcerers with their powers to regrow limbs and eyes used them to grow wings for themselves?"

"No—don't be silly!" Decius protested, hurt by Torio's mocking tone. At fifteen, he was still fighting to be taken seriously.

"Hey—I'm sorry," said Torio. "Decius, it's just that you don't understand the limitations of Adept powers yet. Talk to Master Lenardo and Master Clement about Reading for some of the Lords Adept. You're good enough to do most of what they require, and it will give you a better idea of just how limited an Adept's powers are when you see someone like Wulfston or Aradia collapse after an Adept trick that uses up all their reserves. If you knew how much energy it took to lift something against gravity even for just a moment, you'd realize why flying is impossible."

"Yeah ... I know," Decius said grudgingly. "But—how can you be sure there aren't Adepts somewhere with even *more* powers than Wulfston or Aradia?"

"You're right—I *don't* know," Torio conceded. No one understood exactly how Adept powers worked, for an Adept using them was unReadable. Even Readers who had learned Adept tricks, like Lenardo and Melissa, found that they could not Read at the same time they were applying Adept power.

When the two boys had finished their bath, they dressed in familiar Aventine-style tunics, the warmweather garb Lenardo had popularized in his lands. Torio still felt more comfortable in such clothes than in the silk shirts, hose, and tabards of the savage style.

Decius still wore the plain white linen tunic of a Reader in training, while Torio's was green silk, edged in gold embroidery—a concession to his position as a savage lord. He would have preferred to dress in the black-edged white tunic indicative of a Reader who had reached one of the upper ranks.

Master Clement still wore the robes of a Master

Reader—scarlet cloak over a black-banded white tunic—every day. Lenardo, who had the right to them as well, wore them only on ceremonial occasions.

At nineteen, Torio knew it was better to follow Lenardo's example than Master Clement's, for there was no denying that the world had changed.

Lords Adept had no rules for clothing except richness, it appeared. As their powers made them individualistic, their garb was idiosyncratic—just as Readers dressed alike because their powers united them rather than setting them apart from one another.

Only it's all the same power, Torio reminded himself as he entered Lenardo's house and Read Melissa waiting for him in the courtyard.

"Decius, Melissa's—"

"I know," the younger boy told him. "Go on and get all silly with her. You don't have to worry that *I'll* Read what you're doing!"

In another year or so you'll understand, thought Torio to himself, wondering if Master Clement was trying to stem that awakening in Decius. He had beaten it out of the young Lenardo, Torio had once Read to his utter astonishment. He had never known the gentle Master Reader to use physical punishment on any other student. Despite his efforts, the desire had merely lain dormant in Lenardo until he met Aradia.

Torio had experienced the vague yearnings of adolescence some years ago, too, but he had sublimated them until he had met Melissa last year. Now . . . neither of them knew how to achieve what they wanted. Marriage, they were sure—but when? They were young enough to wait, but also young enough not to want to. Had they not both been brought up in the segregated disciplines of the Academy system, they might simply have followed their inclinations by now.

But both had desires beyond those of the flesh. Torio's Reading abilities were growing at a rate which astonished the Master Readers. While Melissa's Reading talent was maturing only at the normal rate for her age and potential, she had added Adept powers which were growing daily.

The wisdom of both Readers and Adepts who tried to advise the young couple was to wait until their growth spurt had reached its peak before consummating their physical desires.

Thus it was easier for them to be apart most of the time. Nonetheless, Torio went eagerly to the sheltered bench in the courtyard where Melissa waited.

She was a slender young woman with a heart-shaped face and dark hair whose natural curl asserted itself in soft wisps about her face. Spring sunshine had already brought out the freckles across her nose, and she appeared healthy and contented and happy to see him.

They Read each other without words for a moment. Then Torio took Melissa into his arms. Both stopped Reading, to assure their privacy. That left Torio blind, but his other senses were thoroughly saturated with the feel, taste, and scent of Melissa.

They kissed until both were satisfied that they were really together, then sat down side by side, Torio's arm around Melissa, her head on his shoulder.

"I'm so glad you're here," she told him. "I heard what happened yesterday."

"Let's not talk about that," said Torio. "How are you? How are your healing techniques progressing?"

"Steadily. Torio, I don't understand why you can't learn Adept powers. If those attackers had succeeded in killing Wulfston yesterday, you'd have been helpless." She shuddered.

"I haven't forgotten how to use a sword," he reminded her.

"Against people who can stop your heart at a distance?"

"I know. But if you had felt those people burning to death as I did . . . perhaps you wouldn't be so eager to increase your Adept powers."

She nodded against his shoulder. "The Lords Adept have traditionally used their powers for destruction—even someone as thoughtful as Wulfston does it instinctively when his life is threatened. But when those powers are turned to healing . . . Torio, do you remember Zanos?"

"You, too? Decius was just chattering about him. What's going on?"

"Zanos and his wife Astra came with Lilith, and we had a long talk last night. You know, Lilith has set apart some of her lands for Zanos and Astra to rule—they each have both Reading and Adept powers. But Zanos isn't ready to settle down here in the Savage Empire until he goes back to his homeland, which he hasn't seen in over twenty years."

"The home of the Master Sorcerers?" Torio asked.

"Yes!" Melissa said eagerly. "Madura. It's a group of large islands, far in the northern sea. Zanos wants to see if his village is still there, and if any of his kinfolk are still living."

"So why shouldn't he go and see if he wants to? Melissa, we're not trying to hold people who don't want to stay here, are we?"

"No—of course Zanos and Astra are free to go. But it will be a long journey. They're looking for people who might want to join their expedition. There could be dangers, so they want as many Adepts and Readers as possible."

"And you want to go," Torio said flatly, firmly quelling the urge to Read her.

He felt Melissa lift her head, and knew she was looking at him. "Yes," she said. "I want to go. Torio, they have healing techniques far beyond anything we know. Here, a baby born blind can be healed, but nothing can be done for someone your age. In Madura—"

"—they can fly, too," he interrupted her.

"Torio, this is serious! Yes, it's hard to filter out the truth from the garbled stories—but we are just *floundering* here, using trial and error to learn how Readers and Adepts can best join their powers. In Madura they already know! So why should it be surprising that they can do things we can't?"

"At least you're a little more logical than Decius," he told her. "But Melissa, you still have so much to learn *here*. Let the adventurous ones go—and if they find the Madurans friendly and willing to trade knowledge and goods, if they have these healing powers you're so eager for, then of course you will go and study in one of their hospitals. But to undertake a long, dangerous journey on the basis of a few exaggerated tales—"

"You sound just like Lenardo!" she said in exasperation. "Torio, you're young—don't you want some adventure in your life? I do. I love you, but I don't want to stay here just because *you're* afraid to stir out of one safe little haven—"

"Just yesterday I was nearly killed in this 'safe little haven'! Melissa, I have had enough adventure in the past two years to last a lifetime. If you want to go with Zanos—"

Suddenly Melissa was no longer leaning against him. He could feel her, still on the bench beside him, sitting bolt upright as she demanded, *"What* did you say?"

At a loss to explain her reaction, he repeated, "I've had enough adventure—"

"No—*after* that."

"I started to say, if you want to go with Zanos, I won't try to stop you except to ask you to think it through with me."

He could feel her eyes boring into him, and let himself Read her. She was staring at him in alarm, Reading him in return. "Torio—I'm sorry. What I said to you was out of line—but you don't even *know* what you said to me!"

"Well, what *did* I say?"

He could feel her fear and concern as she told him, "You broke off in the middle of a sentence. Then you took your arm away from around me, focused your eyes on me the way you do when you're Reading—except that I *knew* you were not seeing me—and then you said, 'Your destiny, Melissa, is to be found in the frozen isle of Madura. Zanos' fate lies not there, but in a land he has never seen, beyond the southern sea.'"

"That's silly," he said. "I don't talk that way, and I'd certainly know if I said any such thing. I'm trying to talk you *out* of going to Madura, so why would I—?"

But he could Read that she had heard him say the very words she claimed—he Read it through her eyes, saw himself, heard his voice speak it.

"By the gods!" he whispered.

"I . . . I think so," whispered Melissa in return.

"Well," said Torio, "if what I said is true, if your destiny truly does lie in Madura—then so does mine!"

Chapter Two

*"P*rophecy!" said Master Clement when Torio and Melissa let him and Lenardo Read their memories of what had happened in the courtyard. "Son, this is a rare gift, and a dangerous one."

"Not so rare," Torio protested. "You have it, Master Lenardo," he appealed.

"No," said Lenardo, who had finally given up on getting Torio to address him by his savage title, "what I have are precognitive flashes. They are incomplete, and often incoherent, but they are scenes, not words, and I do not blank them out."

"They are also always your own experiences," Master Clement reminded him, then turned to Torio. "You, son, have just predicted the future of two *other* people. What you said, although it doesn't tell us much, is a complete thought and certainly comprehensible. A prophet always knows other people's futures, never his own."

Torio shivered. "I don't *want* to know. This isn't like Reading. I don't like it!"

"Why, Torio?" asked Melissa. "Because you told

me it's right for me to go to Madura, even though you don't want me to?"

"No—because I didn't know what I'd said!"

"Master Clement," said Lenardo, "that is not usual, is it? I've never known a Reader with this gift before."

"Nor I," replied the old man. "It has been generations since the last—but no, I do not recall that the prophet cannot hear his own prophecy. Torio, I think you simply refused to hear yourself tell Melissa she will go far away from here."

"What happens if I don't go?" asked Melissa.

"You will go," said Lenardo. "My precognitive flashes are of fated events. They *always* happen, although almost never in the context I expect."

Master Clement added, "Under the circumstances, there is no reason to think Torio is pulling a prank, nor is this gift something he sought, so it is not wishful thinking. Torio, can you tell me my fate?"

"A child in the womb, a voice from the tomb, a generation of gloom if you serve not your doom."

This time Torio heard the words he spoke—yet it was as if they were spoken by someone else. He had no idea where that doggerel verse came from, or what it meant.

"Interesting," said Master Clement. "What about Decius?"

This time Torio was silent. When no involuntary words came, he said, "I guess I don't know."

"Probably because the boy has not yet done enough in life to establish a direction. Or to attract the notice of the gods, as some men would put it. At the present time, nothing in his life is fated."

Melissa protested, "Then you are saying that the gods will send me to Madura whether I want to go or not?"

Lenardo held out his right arm, displaying the dragon's-head brand. "In the days of the white wolf and the red dragon, there will be peace throughout the land. I had never heard that prophecy, Melissa, nor did I know of Aradia and the white wolf that is her symbol before I came to these lands—and yet she and I together are making that prophecy come true."

"And when the moon devoured the sun last year, Tiberium fell, as it was foretold," Master Clement added.

"But we had that one *wrong*," Torio said eagerly. "It wasn't the eclipse. It was when the failed Readers on the Path of the Dark Moon turned against the Emperor, whose symbol was the sun!"

"Misinterpretation is precisely why this gift is so dangerous, son," explained Master Clement. "Look at the damage we did trying to prevent that prophecy from coming true."

"The point," put in Lenardo, "is that the prophecies do come true, no matter how we try to prevent them. Melissa, my limited experience suggests that you would do better to take your journey to Madura with Zanos than to tempt fate by refusing. Your destiny appears to be to become a great healer. If that is so, then you will never be satisfied until you go and learn those techniques the Maduran sorcerers have to offer."

"*If* they will teach you," said Zanos when Melissa and Torio approached him about joining his expedition. "The stories are contradictory," he explained, "and yet Astra's powers say the people who tell them to us are speaking the truth—or what they think is the truth. The Madura I remember was a peaceful land ruled by Master Sorcerers who kept the weather moderate, so that ours was a garden isle. Now, I'm told, they ignore the people's needs, and the climate has become so cold that the whole land is frozen and nothing grows."

"And the healers?" asked Melissa.

They had found Zanos alone in the suite of rooms he shared with his wife Astra, in the guest house reserved for Lilith and her retinue. Zanos still looked very much the gladiator, a huge, strongly muscled man who rarely stayed still for more than a few minutes at a time. His head was crowned with flaming red hair, and he raked it back with his fingers as he paced the room which seemed too small to contain his restless bulk.

"I don't know what's happened to the healers," he told them. "At one time they were supposed to be the greatest in the world—but now I hear they have gone too far, usurping the powers of the gods. First it was restoring life to the dead. Then metamorphosing men into animals. My friends, ever since I left Tiberium I have been inquiring about Madura—and these are the stories I've been told.

"What I have pieced together tells me only one thing for certain: the rulers of Madura have stopped making their people their first priority. Now they live to pursue the limits of their powers . . . while their people live in fear. In fact, the slavers tell me Madurans go eagerly aboard their ships, willing to grasp at any chance to escape."

"Yet you still want to go there?" asked Torio.

"It was my home," Zanos replied. "I cannot rest until I know if my brother survived the raid in which I was taken. And . . . I must know whether Madura could still be my home. All my life I have dreamed of returning. I cannot simply forget that dream; I must *know* whether my fate lies in Madura."

Melissa looked at Torio, but he said nothing. When they left Zanos, she asked, "Why didn't you tell him what you prophesied?"

"Because nothing I could say would stop him from going. He has a legitimate quest, Melissa— what if he does find his brother living miserably under this new rule? Perhaps he can bring him back here, to live in the lands he and Astra will rule."

"And?" she persisted.

"And . . . you must go to Madura. Better with a well-equipped expedition of Readers and Adepts than in some way we might regret. Besides, if these things I say prove true, then Zanos will have to return safely—and therefore so will you and I."

Once it was decided on, plans for the expedition moved quickly—but it was only a minor concern of the Readers and Adepts who had gathered in Zendi.

In the past year, Lenardo and Aradia had had to put down an attempted takeover of their new government by what was left of the Aventine army, and put an end to the corrupt practices of Readers who had been a small but powerful core within the Aventine Empire. Their leaders might have died in the earthquake that toppled Tiberium, but having once broken their Reader's Oaths they went right on Reading people's private affairs and using what they discovered to extort money or favors.

Ultimately, Lenardo had had no choice but to make examples of the worst of them in a public execution. The others were scattered to menial positions in Academies now governed by Master Readers who had sworn loyalty to their vows a second time, under Oath of Truth before Lenardo and Master Clement.

Lenardo's increased powers meant that not even the most powerful Master Reader could lie to him, but it was Master Clement the other Readers trusted. Despite his protests that Lenardo had the greatest Reading powers ever known, Clement was elected Master of Masters, head of the Council of Master Readers. That, to Torio's mind, was the best decision they had made in years.

Now that the upper ranks of Readers could be trusted once again, they were able to determine how best to use the lesser Readers on the Path of the Dark Moon. Most of those who had not been involved in the attack on Tiberium had simply continued with their assignments as scouts, messengers, midwives, and general finders of things lost.

There were thousands of such people, willing to accept the rule of the new Council of Masters— but there were also hundreds who now knew that they possessed minor Adept powers as well as their small Reading ability. Most of those who had joined in the group-mind that took on a life of its own to destroy Tiberium had spent the year since coping with guilt.

Not only corrupt senators had died, but innocent men as well; not only Master Portia and other

Master Readers who had lent their powers to poli-
ticians and criminals, but other Readers who had
honestly done nothing but obey the Masters to
whom they had sworn loyalty; not only the tyran-
nical royal family, but also hundreds of soldiers
who had been doing nothing but their duty, and
equal numbers of ordinary Aventine citizens out
to watch the Emperor review his troops.

The belief that misusing one's powers weakened
them was such a basic tenet of Academy teaching
that many of the minor Readers in that destruc-
tive group-mind found themselves mind-blind af-
terward. That was a normal temporary effect of
using Adept power, but for these Readers it continued, because they believed themselves no longer
worthy to be Readers at all.

Within the past year, many had been brought
gently back to their original small powers, and
some were brave enough to experiment with Adept powers for healing or other positive purpose.
But others had given up, and were trying to find a
place for themselves as ordinary people with no
special powers at all.

Because of the widespread corruption and re-
bellion in what had been the Aventine Empire,
the savage alliance had allowed little movement
across the old border. After a year of savage rule
little different for most people from what they
had experienced under the Emperor, it was time
to allow more freedom to travel.

Readers on the Path of the Dark Moon, however, were astonished to be *offered* new assignments, instead of merely being informed by the
Council of Masters that they were being sent to a
different place. Both Wulfston and Lilith wanted

to set up relays of Readers in their lands, to transmit messages both more quickly and more privately than the watchers did with their code of flashing lights.

It still frightened many of these minor Readers to find the Lords Adept unReadable. But they could Read Lenardo, Master Clement, Torio, or Melissa—and they reassured them of the Adepts' good intentions.

Soon it was settled who would go to Wulfston's lands—but the Lord Adept was shocked when Torio told him he would not be returning.

"But why, Torio?" Wulfston asked. "Have I offended you in some way?"

Torio shut out the vision of the hill bandits burning to death. "No, not at all. I consider you a valued friend, Wulfston, and I hope to work with you again when I return."

"Return? Where are you going?"

"To Madura with Zanos and Astra ... and Melissa."

"I see. But that's not all, is it?"

"What do you mean?" Torio Read Wulfston curiously, trying once again to detect some sign that the Adept was actually Reading. His sensitivity at times made any other conclusion seem impossible, yet once more Torio could feel nothing when he tried to engage Wulfston's mind.

"Torio, you have been avoiding me ever since we arrived in Zendi—and even before we got here, you hardly talked to me on the last day's ride. I know that you suffered terribly when I burned those bandits ... but you've been working with Adepts long enough to know that I had no choice."

"I know," Torio admitted. "You did what you

had to, but what you had to do, what you *could* do,
was so terrible. I understand why you can't learn
to Read, Wulfston. If you once Read the effects of
an Adept trick like that one, you would never be
able to do it again. And in a similar situation,
you'd be killed."

"Or I might be able to Read how to avoid getting killed without causing my attackers so much
pain," Wulfston replied. "Adepts are not callous,
Torio—at least not all of us are."

"Oh, Wulfston—I *know* that!" said Torio, horribly embarrassed that his friend could think he
thought ill of him. "It's not you—it's me. I still
don't know what I'm supposed to be—and I guess
that's why I can't learn Adept powers, either. I'm
terrified of what I might do with them. And then
just when I'm confused enough already, I have to
develop this new power—"

"What new power? Show me!" said Wulfston,
obviously expecting some evidence that Torio was
indeed starting to develop the power of mind over
matter.

But at the Adept's direct demand, Torio found
himself once more speaking words whose source
he did not know. "Your fate is linked with Lenardo's—but it is your own destiny you will seek far
away, only to find where you began."

"What?" Wulfston stared at him, puzzled.

Torio shrugged. "That's it. When people ask
me their fate, I suddenly tell them something.
Don't ask me what it means, though."

"Well, I already know my fate is linked with
Lenardo's. Ever since he helped Aradia and me
bring our father out of his coma, it's been obvious
that we share a destiny. He seemed to be my

brother even before he married Aradia. But seeking my destiny far away—does that mean I'm supposed to go with you to Madura?"

"No," said Torio, again not knowing where the word came from.

"For someone who's confused about his own fate, you certainly sound positive about other people's!"

"I don't *feel* positive," Torio explained. "This isn't like Reading, Wulfston. All I know is the words as they come, and nothing more about them. And I wish people would stop asking me that kind of question—it's frightening when I blurt out the answer, whether I want to or not."

"You're right that I can't leave my people at this point," Wulfston agreed. "I suppose if Melissa's going, there's no stopping you, is there?"

"No, there's not."

"Then go with my best wishes, Torio—and may the gods protect you."

Before the troop of Readers and Adepts could begin their journey to Madura, though, there was one more task to complete. The hill bandits were growing restless in their camp, and before they dispersed the savage alliance wanted to make certain they did not again consider an attack on any of their members. So a small group of Readers and Adepts set out to show them just how foolish such a move would be.

Lenardo and Aradia led the expedition—not because their tremendous powers were necessary to the plan, but because both were tired of staying in Zendi to arbitrate political and social disputes.

They jumped eagerly at the chance to ride out into the countryside.

Lilith rode with them, paired with Lenardo's adopted daughter Julia, whose Reading powers were quite amazing for an eleven-year-old. Lilith's son Ivorn, whose Adept powers were developing strongly, was close in age to Decius, and the two boys were partners for the occasion.

Zanos and Astra, Melissa and Torio completed their numbers, for Wulfston had returned to his lands two days before.

Ten people rode out against two hundred outlaws, taking no army, no retinue. Their point was precisely to show that the small group could control such large numbers.

Their arrival was perfectly timed. Two of the dead bandits' horses had found their way back to the camp, prompting the outlaws to send out scouts—who returned to report all the attackers dead while the small party from Zendi had still not entered the area covered by the lookouts for the outlaw camp.

Of the ten, only Lilith and Ivorn could not Read at all. The rest depended on Lenardo's powers, for while Adept powers could be joined, a group of minor Adepts equaling the powers of a Lord Adept, Reading powers did not combine. Other Readers, though, could link minds with the most powerful Reader in the party, and Read everything he could.

Lenardo was the most powerful Reader in the history of the Aventine Academy system—although the incredible growth of his powers had come only in the past two years, after he had left that system to interact with the savages. He could Read over great distances without leaving his body, and could discern the finest of distinctions in things so small as to be invisible to the eye. Not even other Master Readers could get a lie past him, and he had achieved the legendary ability to Read without being Read in return.

And besides all that, he had learned to use Adept powers—at least to a limited extent, just as Aradia had learned to Read, although with little distance or discernment. As she exceeded the abilities of any Adept in memory, together they made the most formidable pair ever to rule in the savage lands. Fortunately, neither of them had been raised to be a tyrant, and together they were working toward a government that would allow their people some say in their lives without thinking their leaders vulnerable.

This small expedition would surely become part of the legend they were building.

The outlaw camp was in a ferment of activity as the news spread that their Adepts had died trying to take Wulfston. Torio and Melissa circled to the east of the camp as Lenardo and Aradia moved ahead to take up positions to the north. Zanos and Astra led the others around to the west, and within an hour they were all in position, linked easily by the eight Readers.

Then they moved deliberately on the camp lookouts. Zanos and Astra slid off their horses, crept up on three men watching the trail below, and netted them in a seine such as fishermen used—or gladiators in the arena. While they were securing them in a hopeless tangle, confiscating knives and swords which might cut through the net, Aradia and Lilith were simply putting several other guards to sleep.

Being bombarded with the images of all this happening at once was somewhat disconcerting, but Lenardo had become accustomed to assimilating so much sensory data, and helped the other Readers focus.

Torio and Melissa crept up on a man and two women, whose dog raised its hackles and began to growl. //Wulfston would be able to calm him,// observed Torio.

"Wassa matter, boy?" one of the women asked suspiciously—but the dog turned from growling to whining, wagging its tail and butting her leg with its head. And when she reached down to pat it, she toppled on over, asleep at her post. The man jumped up, but collapsed in his turn, as did the other woman as she turned to flee, caught as she was drawing breath to shout a warning.

By the time Torio and Melissa had secured their prisoners so they would not be able to move when they woke, all the other guards had been similarly dispatched. The party from Zendi moved in on the camp from every side.

They announced their presence with a circle of flame, shooting out of the ground all around the outlaw camp. People shouted and ran, dogs barked, horses reared and screamed.

The flames disappeared as if they had never been—but the moment a hastily loaded wagon bolted, new flames shot up before the horses. They bucked, upsetting the wagon and spilling people and belongings in a tangled heap.

The Readers and Adepts moved in, thunderbolts and sheets of flame preceding them, driving the bandits inexorably into a knot of frightened people in the center of the small valley. They moved between the shelters and wagons, leaving them on the perimeter, while the people were herded like sheep into a cluster where they could all hear what they were told.

"Some of your people," Lenardo shouted, "came into our lands and attacked two of ours—a Reader and a Lord Adept. They learned what powers we have—and that we will not allow such attacks on ourselves and our people. Now *you* must learn!"

The smell of fear sweat clogged Torio's nostrils. Almost two hundred people huddled, prepared to die horribly. Children wailed, parents having no words to comfort them. They were helpless, they knew it, and they were terrified.

All but one boy—no, girl—who turned to face Lenardo defiantly. She said nothing, but her mind spoke resignation rather than fear, standing out clearly against the miasma of sick terror behind her. And there was something else—her resignation was not because she felt she deserved to die, but because she felt that the whole world was like—

Torio could not Read her specific thoughts against the images of horrible pain and death flowing through the minds of all the other people. They were allowed to stew for long moments before Lenardo spoke again.

"You recognize that we can easily kill you?"

Frightened eyes looked all around the circle, as people clung to one another, shivered, and nodded.

"You see how many of us there are? Only ten— but we are both Readers and Adepts. Together, we cannot be defeated!"

Despair settled over the huddled outlaws, as they assumed the delay meant their captors planned to torture them before they killed them. Again that one girl's resignation stood out from the despair of the rest.

But then Lenardo added, "We do not plan to kill you."

Heads snapped to attention; minds surged with hope and suspicion.

"We know what you are thinking," Lenardo continued. "You can no longer plan a sneak attack on a Lord Adept in the Savage Empire—for there will always be Readers to see that no secret plan can be implemented. Nor can you commit crimes against our citizens—your guilt will be Read. If you want to become honest citizens and work for a living, you may return with us to Zendi—but be warned that it will take you a long while to earn our trust.

"But if you wish to remain outside the law, then remain *outside our borders!* If any of you are caught trying to harm our people in any way, you *will* be executed—publicly, as an example to others. Do you understand?"

They didn't quite believe him—Torio Read the usual disbelief that such a powerful Lord could show mercy, which most of these people still regarded as a weakness. Still, relief grew, and he could Read some of them, especially families with children, whispering to one another that this was their chance to leave the outlaw life. Surely whatever work the Lord of Zendi assigned them could not be worse than the short, uncertain lives of outlaws.

To complete the impression, the Readers and

Adepts broke their circle and gathered on either side of Lenardo and Aradia.

The cowed bandits hesitantly left their huddle and returned to their campsites, those closest to the gathered Readers and Adepts last, as if they were afraid moving would attract notice and perhaps arbitrary punishment. But several plucked up their courage and actually came forward to kneel before Lenardo and Aradia. "Me lord, me lady," said the woman who appeared to lead them, "my man was one o' them what you killed—please, me lord, lemme work 'n' take care o' me kids!"

"Of course," Lenardo said gently. "Come back to Zendi. There is plenty of work for willing hands."

The girl Torio had noticed before watched skeptically. Now she gave a snort of disgust, and spat out something in a language he didn't know—all he could Read was that it was one of those oaths so vile that the users forget what the words originally meant, passing them from generation to generation as words taboo in themselves.

But Zanos strode forward. "You there—boy! You're from Madura!"

//She's a girl,// Torio Read Astra tell her husband.

Only then did Torio really "look" at the girl. She was somewhere about his own age, but because she was dressed as a boy she looked younger. Her hair, dirty and chopped off raggedly, was a slightly darker red than Zanos', and her eyes were a clear green. The beauty of her sculpted face beneath the dirt and the hair hanging in her eyes showed him at once why she had hidden her sex while living among these ruffians.

"Lass," Zanos was saying more gently, in his native language. The concepts were concrete, making it easy for Torio to Read what he was saying even though he did not know Maduran. "Why did you come away from Madura? What are you doing among these outlaws? You are from my homeland, girl—tell me, how long ago were you last there?"

Her green eyes flashed fire as she spat back, "Sorcerer! You think you'll take me back to Maldek? I'll kill myself first!"

"What? Who is Maldek? Child, it is more than twenty years since I was stolen away from Madura," Zanos told her. "I seek to find out whether any of my kin survived the raid in which I was taken."

"Why should I believe you?" the girl demanded.

He didn't have an answer, but his wife did. Astra turned to those bandits who had come forward to indicate willingness to return to Zendi and asked in the savage language, pointing to Zanos, "Is there anyone among you who knows who this man is?"

That drew blank stares from all but one man, who squinted at the red-haired giant and replied in the same language but with an Aventine accent, "I remember—I seen him in the arena oncet. That's Zanos the Gladiator."

"And where did you see him?"

"Adigia—afore Drakonius took the last bit o' land right where we was farmin'. That journey t'see the games was the last time me an' my wife had a happy time t'gether."

"You see?" Astra said to the girl. "Zanos was inside the Aventine Empire for the past twenty years, just as he told you."

"So what?" asked the girl.

"So I had nothing to do with what is happening

in Madura now," Zanos replied. "Please, lass, if you were there recently, tell me what is happening in my homeland."

Zanos and Astra, Torio and Melissa took the girl—who had little to pack in the way of possessions—aside to talk while the rest of the bandits were loading their horses and wagons.

"What is your name?" Zanos asked.

The girl looked resentfully at Astra, and said aloud what her mind had already told the Readers: "Dirdra."

"Why did you leave Madura?"

"I told you. To escape Maldek."

When she spoke the name, Torio Read a combination of fear, revulsion, anger, and despair.

"What did this Maldek do to you, Dirdra, to make you hate him so?" Astra spoke gently, adding, "No—not to you, was it? To someone you love."

Forced to think about something she had thrust to the back of her mind, Dirdra lost some of her toughness. Tears burned behind her eyes, and one escaped to slide down her cheek. "My brother," she said in a tight voice. "Maldek destroyed him."

"Killed him?" Zanos asked before the better Readers could stop him.

"No," Dirdra replied. "I wish he had. And I couldn't—couldn't stop him from—"

A painful sob heaved the girl's chest. Then, "He's still alive!" she choked out. "Why didn't I have the strength to kill him rather than let him live that way?"

Torio Read odd flashes of a shadowed, bent figure as Dirdra fought her own memories, refusing the agony of seeing clearly what her brother had become. But all the Readers—even Zanos, Reading with Astra—recognized that Maldek had crippled him in some terrible manner.

It was Melissa who asked, "Why?"

"Maldek wanted me," the girl replied. "He . . . wanted me awake and willing, not mind-forced, not orbu."

"Orbu?" asked Zanos, not knowing the word in what was supposed to be his native language.

Dirdra said something else that Torio could not understand because Zanos didn't. With the strange words, though, came images—a beautiful young woman, a handsome young man, physically per- fect but without the spark of intelligence in their eyes. They were dolls or puppets, yet they were living flesh and moved with human grace.

It was a chamber of a castle in which Dirdra— held still and silent by Adept power—was forced to stand and watch. The pair of exquisitely beauti- ful automatons approached the man who reclined on the couch: Maldek.

Torio was startled to see that he was young— somehow he had expected an aged drooling lecher. Rather, Maldek appeared to be in his thirties, and a fine specimen of manhood. His broad shoulders were exaggerated by a tabard built out beyond them—yet he would not have needed that extra width. He was built almost as powerfully as Zanos.

His silver-encrusted black tabard was cut short, to reveal long, well-formed legs to which his black hose gave full display. He posed, one leg bent, as physically beautiful as the pair before him—but alive, charged with vitality.

His hair was thick, and darker than the Maduran norm, showing red glints in the torchlight, but his

eyes were Maduran blue, fringed with thick black
lashes. Lest the eyes seem effeminate, his jaw was
square and firm. Otherwise his features were finely
chiseled, and he was clean-shaven to display them.

Torio recognized that Dirdra felt a powerful
physical attraction to Maldek, but what she knew
of his character caused her to deny it. The scene
she was remembering showed why.

Maldek beckoned the young man and woman
forward. They were dressed only in loose smocks,
and at his command dropped them, standing in
naked glory.

The woman was golden blond, perfectly formed
from ample but youthfully firm breasts through
slender waist to hips just full enough to balance in
lovely curves above long, slender legs.

The man had the more typically Maduran reddish hair, on the sandy side. He, too, had been
chosen at the peak moment of youth verging on
maturity, a strong body, well proportioned and
toned with exercise.

At Maldek's command, the man began to stroke
and fondle the woman. Both of them became ex-
cited, sweat sheening their bodies—but their eyes
remained dead.

Suddenly Maldek snapped his fingers. Although
aroused and unsatisfied, the young man instantly
let go of the woman. Dropping his arms to his
sides, he turned and with stiff, reluctant steps left
the room.

The woman took one step after him, holding
out her arms with a wordless cry of disappointment. Then, although Maldek did not speak, she
turned and walked seductively toward the couch.

Maldek rose. Each move an eager caress, the

woman began to remove his clothes, kissing his skin as she exposed it.

Dirdra tried to close her eyes, to turn her head away, but Maldek's power held her helpless. His beautiful but cold eyes fixed on her over the shoulder of the woman undressing him.

"You see what you can have, Dirdra? Come to me freely; let us enjoy our youth and health together. Enjoy, Dirdra. Know the pleasure only a Master Sorcerer can give."

At his words, a hot wave of arousal spread upward from Dirdra's loins. She blushed in agonized embarrassment as she recognized her body's yearning—

"No! Ohhh . . . no!"

Dirdra's scream was in the present—at the time she was remembering, Maldek had held her powerless to speak, Reading her reactions with evil glee.

Now she stared at the four Readers. "You're just like him—making me remember! Feasting on my thoughts!" She clapped her hands to the sides of her head, but being neither Reader nor Adept she could not close off her thoughts.

Dirdra's green eyes darted fire as she shouted, "I don't care anymore! I'll kill myself before I submit! If you want me then, you'll have nothing but an orbu!"

Chapter Three

"*D*irdra," said Zanos, "no one here wants to hurt you. We seek information, that's all."

"It was my fault," said Astra in halting Maduran, and Torio realized that she had stopped Reading. "My Reading powers are difficult to control—on the wave of your emotion, I could not help Reading your memory, and that broadcast it to everyone else. Dirdra—please forgive me."

The green eyes studied her warily. "Why should I trust you?"

"You have no reason to," Astra replied truthfully.

"But I'm Maduran, like you," said Zanos.

"So is Maldek!" Dirdra spat.

"Bu I'd never heard of him before today. I was stolen away from my home when I was much younger than you."

"Then you were fortunate," Dirdra said flatly. "Those who rule now would kill you—they will have no rivals in the powers of sorcery!"

"Like Drakonius," Torio put in. "But Dirdra, not all Adepts are like Maldek. How long have you been here in the Savage Empire?" His command of the savage language was excellent by now, but he would always speak it with an Aventine accent.

Dirdra answered in the same language with a Maduran accent, but it was not linguistic differences which confused her. "What is the Savage Empire?"

"These lands," Torio replied. "The lands which once belonged to Drakonius, Nerius, and Lilith—and the Aventine Empire, which is no more. It is now joined into one unit—and how could you not know that?"

"I know you defeated Drakonius," Dirdra replied. "That story I heard everywhere in my travels—and how there was a prophecy about peace in the lands of the white wolf and the red dragon. That is why I tried to get to Zendi . . . but as I got closer, I heard new stories—how you made earthquakes, not caring who they killed. That's how you took the Aventine Empire, isn't it? You destroyed the capital city—the Emperor and his whole family—leaving no one but you to rule." Her green eyes dared them to deny it . . . but of course they could not.

"I know you will not believe it, Dirdra," Melissa said at last, "but we were trying to *prevent* the earthquake. We learned that what has been foretold cannot be stopped."

"Foretold?" Dirdra asked. "The earthquake was foredoomed?" For some reason, this suggestion changed the girl's attitude.

"When the moon devours the sun," Melissa quoted the prophecy, "the earth will devour

Tiberium—and it did, despite everything we tried to prevent it."

"And . . . is not your Lord Lenardo the red dragon?" Dirdra asked.

"That is his symbol," Torio told her, "and Aradia—his wife—the white wolf is hers."

"Then perhaps in this Savage Empire," said the girl, "I truly will find the peace I have sought all the way from Madura!"

Over the next few days, Torio and Melissa spent much of their time with Zanos and Astra, planning the expedition to Madura. They would travel by sea, taking ship at Dragon's Mouth, the natural harbor in Wulfston's territory.

Zanos was frustrated that Dirdra would have nothing to do with their plans. "She could tell us so much!"

But the young Maduran woman discarded her boy's clothes for dresses the moment she saw that it was safe for women to display their beauty in Zendi—for beauty she had aplenty. Even her shorn hair could not mar the perfection of her translucent skin, delicate bone structure, and beautiful eyes—and when her hair was clean and brushed softly out around her face, it glowed a soft, rich auburn.

Dirdra was a weaver, and quickly obtained employment when she displayed her skills before the newly formed guild. The craft guilds, loosely based on the Academy system, took the place of the family units Drakonius had destroyed; only time would tell if they would develop into a permanent system for passing down vital knowledge from one generation to another.

So Zanos mulled over whatever outdated maps of Madura he could obtain, and tried to make adequate plans. The northern isles were too far for any Reader to attempt to visit out of body—even Lenardo. The gladiator took heart from the fact that his home village was marked on two of the maps . . . and the others refrained from pointing out that those particular maps could have been older than he was.

Melissa was eager for the journey—so much so that it began to grate on Torio's nerves after a time. Finally he went to talk to Lenardo.

"Are you brooding again?" his mentor asked. "Grow up, Torio. If you don't want to go adventuring, stay home, but don't blame Melissa for wanting to learn more of what she can do with her powers."

"And don't you give me that same advice again!" Torio snapped. "I *am* trying to conquer my powers." They were in Lenardo's office again, not Reading for privacy. Although that left Torio blind, he had learned in recent months to rely on different clues, as other blind persons did.

Now he stood and faced Lenardo. "Why do I have to be a leader?" he asked. "Why do I have to rule lands? There are other things a man can do with his life—there was nothing wrong with the Aventine Academy system for Readers except that it kept those Readers who were *meant* for leadership, like you, from having power. And that led to corruption in Readers like Portia, who could not gain power except through devious means.

"But Master Lenardo, not every Reader was born to rule! And the more I watch you, Aradia, Wulfston—the less I feel I can ever be like you.

Why can't I just be a Reader? Why do I have to be a lord?"

He could feel Lenardo staring at him. Then the older man said, "I never really thought about it, Torio. *I* found myself when Aradia gave me lands to rule—but you don't have to follow in my footsteps. It's too bad that you cannot prophesy your own destiny—but I will certainly stop trying to tell you what it ought to be."

Torio unexpectedly felt himself blushing. He had fought, even killed in battle—but never before had he stood up angrily to someone in authority over him. It was the first time he realized that Lenardo no longer had such authority. They were both grown men now—equals—and Lenardo freely acknowledged it. It was disconcerting, but it also gave him a strange new sense of pride.

Then, "I'm sorry," he said. "I didn't mean to shout at you, Master Lenardo. You're not the one causing my frustration."

"Melissa?" the older man asked.

"Yes. No. It's—just when I think I'm discovering what to do with my life, the gods drop some other power on me that I didn't ask for and don't want. My own words are sending the woman I love away, Master. What can I do but go with her?"

"You could try living your *own* life, Torio," Lenardo suggested. "Do you realize that today is the first time I've ever seen you talk back to someone you respect? You've always been too much of a good boy."

"What do you mean?"

"At the Academy, you never got into mischief—I

mean serious mischief, not daydreaming and forgetting your lessons."

"You caught me gambling with the stable boys
once," Torio reminded him.

"Yes—because you were angry with me, not because it was something you wanted to do. Torio,
you don't act, you *re*act. I'm not pleased that you're
going on this journey to follow Melissa, but I
won't try to stop you. Perhaps along the way you
may learn some leadership, and stop being afraid
to take the authority your powers have earned
you. We *need* leaders—so perhaps by the time you
come back you'll be ready to take responsibility
for your own people."

Torio left his meeting with Lenardo feeling
pleased that his teacher recognized him as an adult.
However, he still had no answer to what he was to
do with his life. Perhaps when he and Melissa
returned from Madura he should try teaching in
Master Clement's new Academy. Or perhaps when
they discovered what destiny drew Melissa to the
frozen isles, he would find his own as well.

So he returned to his room, still the same small,
simply furnished room he preferred. There would
always be a place for him in Lenardo's home—
even after their confrontation, he did not have to
ask. But there were guest houses now, where
Wulfston and Lilith and other dignitaries stayed
when they visited Zendi. Lenardo's villa was no
longer sparsely furnished, either—lavish furnishings filled the public rooms, works of art were
scattered here and there, and the suite of rooms
Lenardo shared with Aradia was rich with silks,
satins, and velvets.

Decius came to the door. "Torio, will you help

me persuade Master Clement to let me go with you to Madura? He thinks I'm a cripple—even after I helped him escape out of the Aventine Empire!"

"No he doesn't, Decius," Torio assured the boy. "No one can possibly think that about you—but you are young. You'll have plenty of time in your life for adventuring. Master Clement is old—and he needs you, although he'd never admit it."

"What do you mean?" Decius asked.

"You've already said it. He could never have escaped the empire without your help."

"Well—he was all bent up with rheumatism then. The Adepts here cured that."

"Yes, but they can't cure old age. Decius, of all the boys in the Adigia Academy, you are the only one Master Clement could confide in when Portia threatened him. He *trusts* you—and he needs your help in his new Academy here in Zendi. And surely you know how much he has to teach you about Reading?"

"Yes, but—"

"You are on the brink of the first great growth of your powers. There will be no Master Readers on our journey—Astra, Melissa, and I are only Magisters. None of us has the years of experience Master Clement has ... and he won't be here forever. There will be the whole world out there for you to go adventuring in after you have achieved the rank of Magister—and you will do so easily under Master Clement's tutelage. But if you leave now, you will miss the opportunity to have the Master of Masters' guidance at this crucial time. And ... you do not understand right now how very much he will rely on you during the difficulties to come."

Decius stared at him. "Is that . . . one of your prophecies?"

He hadn't been able to say anything about Decius when Master Clement had asked him—but now he knew, without knowing how he knew, that Decius was involved in Master Clement's destiny. "Yes—I think it is, Decius. I can't tell you any more than that, though. You must stay in Zendi, for Master Clement's sake."

The boy sighed. "All right—but you have to promise, if it's true that the Maduran sorcerers can make limbs regrow, that you'll tell me, so I can go—"

"You don't think we would keep that kind of information to ourselves, do you? Melissa is going because she wants to learn to do it if it's true—so it may just be that she will come back able to heal you!"

"Is *that* a prophecy?"

"No. It's just a speculation. Now come and help me figure out how to get all of the stuff I want to take along into this one bag. I think it will take Adept power!"

"I'm no Adept, but I know the trick that will do it," Decius replied.

"Oh? Show me!"

Torio had hung on the pegs in his room woolen tunics and leggings such as were worn here in the dead of winter. It was said to be cold even in the summer in Madura—and they might well be there through the winter.

Decius picked one set of woolen undergarments and a heavy cloak off the pegs and tossed them on the bed. "There. You take those for when you first arrive—and for the rest . . . pack money!"

Torio laughed—and realized that the boy was right. But after Decius had gone, he thought about their conversation, and wondered—was it because he was leaving that Decius was now involved in Master Clement's destiny? Was he taking over a role meant for Torio?

Two years ago, Torio had praised Decius' swordsmanship—and the boy had thought himself ready to defend his Academy. Without the knowledge or permission of the Master Readers he had joined the battle—and lost his leg. And perhaps the main reason for Torio's guilt was the fact that Decius had never once blamed him.

What am I exposing him to this time? Torio wondered. A voice from the tomb? A generation of gloom? What did it mean? What good was it to be a prophet if he couldn't understand his own prophecies?

Besides, there was no time set on those strange words. Master Clement was in perfect health now—he could live for ten or even twenty more years, and his "destiny" could occur tomorrow or at the end of his life. Taking Decius away would not avoid his destiny, and would expose him to known hardships and unknown dangers. And it was only common sense that he stay here, where Master Readers could teach him, while he learned to use his growing Reading skills.

Face it, Torio told himself. *Decius will be much better off if you just stay out of his life for a while.*

There was a grand farewell dinner at Lenardo's villa, followed by entertainment. Lenardo's bard retold the stories of the white wolf and the red dragon, the defeat of Drakonius and the fall of Tiberium.

Zanos and Astra were musicians, and now they played while everyone danced. It was a lovely evening . . . and no one let the thought slip out that it might be the last time they would all be together.

In the morning, the train of horses waited outside Lenardo's villa as they said their goodbyes. And just as they were mounting up, Dirdra came down the street, dressed once more in boy's clothes and carrying a knapsack containing her meager possessions.

She approached Zanos and Astra. "My lord . . . my lady—may I beg permission to return with you to Madura?"

"Why now?" demanded Zanos. "You'd have nothing to do with our preparations. Why have you suddenly decided to go now?"

She raised her clear green eyes to his blue ones. "Because . . . I have found that I cannot live at peace with myself in this peaceful land, while I know that my brother suffers in Maldek's power. Lord Zanos, you do not even know if you have kin alive in Madura—but you cannot rest until you find out and free them. So how can I leave a brother I *know* to be suffering? I must free him from Maldek, or die trying."

"Then join us, lass," said Zanos, "and welcome. Your knowledge will be most valuable."

Thus they were five setting out on their journey— no retinue, no servants. Torio, Melissa, and Astra had all grown up as Readers taking care of themselves and never aspiring to have servants. Zanos had aspired—but his servants had betrayed him.

Now he and Astra chose to fend for themselves—
and all agreed that the fewer they were, the faster
they would travel.

Dirdra, having little money, had made most of
her journey from Madura by land. The first part,
from the islands to the mainland, had had to be
by ship—and that was when she had disguised
herself as a boy, so as to pay her way with the few
coins she possessed, rather than with her body.

It had taken her the whole winter to work her
way southward, doing odd jobs for her keep, to
the place where she had found that a peaceful
land could not bring her peace of mind. But she
would say little about what had happened to her
in Maldek's castle, and nothing explicit about what
the sorcerer had done to her brother.

Torio and Melissa were learning the Maduran
language, and Astra was polishing what she had
learned from Zanos. Dirdra avoided Astra, not
trusting her to leave her mind in privacy. Like
many nonReaders, Dirdra seemed to have exaggerated notions of Readers' abilities—but it was
obvious she had learned to avoid attracting attention. It had been Astra who had admitted to broad-
casting her memories to the group of Readers
when they had first met, and although she had
apologized, it would obviously take some time for
her to gain Dirdra's trust.

It occurred to Torio early in the journey to tell
Dirdra he was blind, and therefore Read almost
every moment he was awake. He didn't want her
to find out later and mistrust him . . . but he
didn't expect her reaction.

"You are the one . . . they claim you were raised
from the dead?"

Was that angry lie to haunt him all his life? Lenardo was right—he had reacted, and reacted badly, to Portia's unexpected credulity. And that moment's weakness had brought nothing but trouble.

"Yes, that is said about me," he told Dirdra. "It is not true, though."

She nodded. "It couldn't be. If your Adepts could restore life as you have it, they would not be seeking the knowledge of the Master Sorcerers. This thing that made people think you dead—it caused your blindness?"

"No, I was born blind," Torio explained. "Once I learned to Read, it was no great inconvenience. But two years ago I escaped from the Aventine Empire with Master Lenardo. At the border gate, I knocked the Reader on guard unconscious—so when one of the soldiers shot me, he thought his arrow had gone through my heart.

"It hadn't. I had a very bad wound, but nothing an Adept healer could not easily cure. I don't even have a scar.

"But the border guards reported they had killed me. Portia was Master of Masters among Readers then. When she discovered me alive, she was so surprised that she asked me if I had been raised from the dead. I was angry, and her question seemed so foolish to me that I said yes. I never dreamed she would believe it!"

Dirdra nodded, and stared off toward the distant coastline they paralleled. "Any Master Sorcerer should easily have detected such a lie. Even though you are a sorcerer, too, you are too young to have reached your full powers."

"I'm no sorcerer," said Torio. "I have no Adept powers at all."

Dirdra turned to face him, leaning against the rail. "This division of powers—I do not understand. Once through the land of the Dark Forest, I found only what you call Adepts—no one with the inner sight, although I heard about the Readers in the Aventine Empire, where no one had Adept powers. In Madura someone may have only one or two slight abilities, but anyone as powerful at the inner sight as you are will surely have Adept powers as well."

"We are learning," Torio replied. "Our powers are of the mind . . . and the mind is influenced by what one believes. Perhaps even more so by what an entire society believes. No one in the empire or the savage lands knew until two years ago that it was possible for one person to have both powers."

"But now that you know," Dirdra persisted, "why have you not developed the other side of your powers?"

"I don't know. Perhaps I don't yet truly believe it's possible, even though I see my friends doing it. Or maybe it's that I do not want such ability. I do not want to rule people . . . and it is so easy to misuse such powers."

"In Madura," Dirdra said bitterly, "no Master Sorcerer would worry about such a thing."

"Ah, but they will lose their powers that way," Torio pointed out. "That is no trick of the mind, Dirdra. You said you were surprised I could lie to Portia. So was I—but in misusing her powers she had weakened them. And Drakonius—he became ever more careless of the responsibilities that came with his powers, and we were able to defeat him."

Dirdra sighed. "You are so young."

"And you are so much older and wiser?"

"I have more experience of the world," she replied. "If by misuse of powers, you mean to use other people as you please, with no regard for their suffering, then Maldek misuses his powers daily . . . and yet they grow and grow."

"Perhaps they are concentrated on one thing," Torio offered. "We have heard that your sorcerers have lost control of the climate—that once verdant isles are now frozen wastes."

"That is true," she replied, "but the Master Sorcerer has good reason to fear the heat of the sun. You will see—" She broke off, catching her lower lip between her teeth.

Before Torio could reassure her that no blind person became upset at the mention of sight, Dirdra suddenly said, "Lord Torio, are you seeking the Master Sorcerers to have them restore your sight?"

"No," he replied. "Melissa seeks such knowledge of healing, but not for my sake. But is she chasing rainbows, Dirdra? Could your Master Sorcerers actually do such a thing?"

"Oh, yes. Maldek could do it all by himself . . . if he wished. But do not ask it, my lord. Even if you were no Reader, nothing could be worth the price Maldek would make you pay!"

The long sea journey in close quarters was a time for the adventurers to get to know one another better. Torio and Melissa spent each evening together, talking, watching the stars, arms about each other for warmth against the night wind. Such constant closeness made them desire to be closer still—but what of the consequences?

One evening they dared to discuss it with Zanos and Astra. Driven belowdecks by stinging rain, the four of them huddled into the tiny cabin the married couple shared.

"Yes," said Astra, "both our powers were weakened for a time after we consummated our marriage. In fact, my Reading was nicely controlled during those few weeks—I had to concentrate in order to Read at all, and the bit of Adept power I had acquired disappeared. But it came back."

"So did all my powers," Zanos assured them. "In fact, I think my Adept powers have grown stronger, although I cannot be certain, since I've spent the past year learning from experienced Adepts how to use them more efficiently."

When the younger couple left together, Torio knew that the same thing was on Melissa's mind as was on his. It would take a few weeks to reach Madura, time for weakened powers to return. If they experimented now . . .

Melissa shared a cabin with Dirdra, who made no secret of her femininity despite her boy's clothes—she wore them now, she said, because they were more comfortable for travel than women's skirts. Neither Melissa nor Astra was interested in testing her claims.

Torio had been given the cabin assigned to a Reader if one were aboard to navigate, although the crew of this vessel were accustomed to finding their way without one. There was hardly room to turn around—but that made it all the cozier when he and Melissa were there together. There was no place to sit but on the bunk, which they did, Melissa leaning against Torio, first letting him kiss her, then participating eagerly.

They were stretched out in the cramped quarters, clumsily pulling at one another's clothing, when suddenly the ship lurched, almost throwing them off the bunk.

Both automatically Read for what had happened, and found that they had run into a squall. Nothing particularly dangerous in that, except—

"Islands!" they both exclaimed, and tangled with one another, nearly going down in a heap as they struggled to get out of the cabin and warn the captain.

By the time Torio and Melissa lurched up the ladders to the deck, Astra was already with the captain at the wheel, shouting directions into his ear against the wind.

The two younger Readers retreated, but in the swinging lantern light they wordlessly agreed. Yes, there might be three Readers in their party—for Zanos' powers were not up to the job his wife was doing—but if they put themselves out of commission, that would throw the entire responsibility of Reading onto Astra. It was not only unfair to do so; it was dangerous.

So with one more embrace, they parted—and the next day Torio decided to take his mind off his frustrations and keep himself in condition at the same time by offering to practice swordsmanship with Zanos.

The gladiator first put Astra through a complex lesson, for he insisted his wife be able to handle herself under attack. Torio watched, surprised at how well a woman could perform and wondering what skills she might have achieved if she had begun in childhood, as he had.

When Zanos turned to Torio, he of course saw

a tall, lean young man with nothing like the gladiator's size or strength. A fighter of Zanos' experience, though, did not judge by appearances. Furthermore, he knew that Torio had survived far more battles than the average man his age, so he certainly had some ability.

But it was clear from Zanos' first moves that he expected a swordsman of Astra's skill, with the same advantage of Reading—for he kept himself unReadable, braced to use Adept power although never actually using it.

Torio countered Zanos' opening moves with the standard countermoves; why give the game away in the first moments? He quickly recognized that the older man was putting him through a routine he himself might use in deciding whether to take a young swordsman on as a pupil.

So he was on the alert for the break with routine—and when Zanos suddenly, without rhyme or reason, lifted his arm as if to strike at Torio's neck, the Reader was in under his guard instantly, his blunt practice weapon making a resounding thwack against the padding Zanos wore.

"Very good!" said the gladiator with a grin—and attacked at that same moment.

Torio caught Zanos' sword with his, and used the fighter's own momentum to twist his wrist.

The move would have disarmed any other opponent. Zanos, though, had the sheer brute strength to hang on to his grip and force Torio to disengage before the gladiator reversed the torque on him. Fortunately, the young Reader could sense the tension of the gladiator's muscles preparing for the next move, and keep one step ahead of him.

For although Zanos was amazingly fast for his
size, Torio was faster—he turned the disengage
into a strike at Zanos' thigh before the other man
could bring his sword fully around to parry. This
time it was a stinging slap to bare skin, but Zanos
only laughed in delight.

"By the gods, Torio—I'd hire you for my stable
of fighters any day! Who would expect such fire
under that scholarly exterior?"

And Zanos stopped holding back. Soon he got a
blow in, and continued trying to maneuver the
Reader into positions where the gladiator's strength
was an advantage, while Torio sought to use his
greater speed.

With their differing styles but equal cunning,
they were evenly matched. Their bouts on the
long days of the sea journey often ended in a
draw, both men happily played out.

But there were things Torio could learn from
Zanos. Hand-to-hand fighting, for example, without weapons. Zanos was only too happy to teach
him that, as well as how to use a knife as a weapon.

And Torio, although the youngest of the three
Magister Readers on this journey, was the most
skilled. Astra's wild powers were stronger, but she
still often lacked control, and gladly handed her
husband over to Torio to learn how best to use his
small Reading talent.

So the lengthening days passed as they sailed
out of the Southern Sea and northward along the
shores of strange countries. The ship's captain
knew ports where it was safe to go ashore, take on
water and food, and trade for supplies and trinkets.

At each such stop the sailors had leave to visit
the taverns, while the passengers chafed at the

delay. Finally, though, they accepted that the captain would govern his crew as he thought best, and began to enjoy the occasional day ashore.

Dirdra was not the only refugee who had fled Madura in recent years; the farther north they traveled, the less the language was like the dialects of the savage tongue they were accustomed to, but the easier it was to find someone who spoke Maduran. Eventually they reached a land called Brettonia, where to Torio, Melissa, and Astra the language seemed to be Maduran itself, although Zanos and Dirdra claimed it was simply a related dialect.

It had been nine days since their last stop, for when they passed the land of the Dark Forest, the ship's captain had warned that the people there were hostile to strangers, letting them pass only on the high sea or on the main road Dirdra had traveled. So they had stayed far out to sea, the Readers fascinated at the way the captain navigated by sun and stars when they were out of sight of land.

It was early summer in Brettonia, and everyone was delighted to go ashore. The little port city perched on a cliff above the harbor, and the five adventurers climbed the winding path in search of a bathhouse, fresh fruit and vegetables, and an inn where they could get a good meal rather than the stuff served in the quayside taverns to which the sailors quickly repaired.

Yellow daisies with dark brown centers grew beside the cliff path. Torio picked some and wove them into a garland for Melissa, who thanked him with a kiss.

But she blushed rosily when they found them-

selves in the baths—for the custom here was for
families, or groups of friends such as these obviously were, to bathe together without regard to
sex.

The "bathhouse" was merely a structure at the
opening to some underground mineral springs.
At this time of day there was no one else bathing,
so the attendant rented them soap and towels,
showed them around, and then left them to their
own devices.

Zanos unself-consciously stripped and plunged
into a pool of bubbling water. Astra waited only
until he surfaced, shaking water from his hair and
announcing, "It's warm!" Then she joined her
husband.

But Torio and Melissa had never quite been
naked together. That they were restricting their
Reading lest Astra and Zanos perceive their un-
easiness at a public unveiling only made their shy-
ness more pronounced.

Just as Torio decided the best thing to do was to
be bold, and started taking off his clothes, Dirdra
said, "How can you be embarrassed? You are
Readers—you see everything anyway."

"Certainly not!" replied Melissa. "The rules of
privacy are drilled into us as children."

Dirdra had divested herself of the layers of loose
garments which obscured her figure, and now
stood in nothing but a shirt of soft cotton. "There
are no such rules for Master Sorcerers," she said,
"and when we first met—"

Astra came to the edge of the pool. "How often
must I apologize, Dirdra? There are times when
the only way to control my wild Reading talent is
to brace for Adept powers—but I do not want to

blank out constantly the powers I have relied on since childhood. Please understand that it was entirely my fault that we invaded your privacy when we first met. Torio or Melissa would never do such a thing."

"And I *couldn't*," added Zanos. "I can just barely Read at all—mostly Astra projects to me."

"I promise," said Astra, "that I will never deliberately invade your privacy . . . nor would I use anything I discover against you."

Dirdra looked from Astra to Zanos, then back to Torio and Melissa. "I . . . I know. Just these few weeks—you, with all your powers—you've accepted me, although I have none. Never in all my travels did I find that. Those with power use it to control others—but not you. Lady Astra, you need ask no forgiveness, but"—as Astra drew breath to protest—"I give it as you desire it."

With that, Dirdra slipped off her shirt and plunged into the pool, where Astra hugged her.

Torio and Melissa, of one mind, grasped the moment when attention was diverted from them to throw off the rest of their clothes and dive into the pool.

With three Magister Readers, the group could enjoy the baths without worrying about security. Someone would be sure to notice if anyone else entered the caverns. Nonetheless, their weapons lay ready beside the pool, a precaution Zanos and Astra lived by.

The water was exhilarating: warm and tingling as a brisk massage. It was about shoulder-deep on Torio, deep enough to swim, or just stand and let the currents swirl pleasantly around them.

Melissa and Astra loosed their long hair to wash

it free of salt from their ocean voyage, and soon soap bubbles were added to the natural effervescence of the pool.

The men soaped their hair and beards, too. It was inconvenient to try to shave each day on a journey—and Torio had discovered with secret pleasure that at last he could grow a real man's beard.

When all were clean, Zanos led the charge into a larger cavern, where a small waterfall tumbled over the rocks above them. The cave was open to the sky, bringing a shaft of sunshine to warm them when they emerged shivering from the deep pool at the foot of the cascade.

Zanos discovered that he could climb the rocks to about twice his height, and dive into the pool. When Astra followed, Melissa tugged at Torio's hand. "Come on—let's try it!"

Astra jumped in feet first, but Zanos had dived head first, arms extended. Not to be outdone, even though he had never dived from such a height in his life, Torio tried to copy Zanos' form— and struck the water so hard with his chest and stomach that the breath was knocked out of him.

As he surfaced, gasping, Zanos laughed. "Good try, lad—now you know how *not* to do it!"

Torio managed a grin. Melissa didn't try to dive, just jumped—but when the other four were at the side of the pool, looking up to see what had become of her, Dirdra astonished them all by leaping upward, bending gracefully into a dive as clean and lovely as that of a seabird, and cutting neatly into the water with hardly a splash.

The cascade pool was too cold for them to play in long, but Torio tried two more dives before he finally found the right angle and entered the water cleanly—nothing to Dirdra's grace, but satisfactory to himself.

As they toweled off, Zanos asked Dirdra, "Where did you learn to dive like that? I don't recall the women of our village even learning to swim."

"Where I grew up," she replied, "there were cliffs about a natural harbor—much like the cliffs here, except that they extended farther out into the water. When my brother and I were children, we would climb partway up the cliffs near where the ships anchored. The sailors would throw coins into the water to watch us dive for them."

"That sounds like a dangerous sport for children," observed Astra.

"We were poor," Dirdra replied. "Our parents needed every coin Kwinn and I brought home. We were the oldest children—and now we're the last of our family."

So Kwinn was the brother Dirdra had left in Maldek's power.

Silence fell, as everyone strove not to Read Dirdra's feelings. They pulled on undergarments, and Melissa and Astra sat down in the shaft of sunshine and began to comb their hair.

Torio, doing the Reading exercise called "visualizing" to compensate for his lack of sight, helped Zanos carry the rest of their clothes—along with their weapons—over to where the women sat. He also Read beyond the cavern, as he had done periodically since they had arrived, to see that no other party of bathers was on the way to interrupt them. All he Read were seven burly men climbing the road that passed the bathhouse—some sort of workers, it appeared from the picks, shovels, and poles they carried.

Intending to check in a few minutes to see if baths were what the seven men were coming this way for, Torio returned his attention to the group at the cascade pool—just as Zanos, half dressed, picked up his huge sword and unsheathed it.

"Zanos—what—?"

As Torio opened wide to Reading, certain Zanos could not possibly have noticed something he hadn't, Astra screamed.

Zanos swung the sword—striking at his wife!

But he was clumsy as Torio had never seen him. Astra ducked, and made a leap toward her own weapon.

But Torio was right there, his sword immediately at the ready as Zanos turned and grabbed Dirdra.

The astonished Maduran woman was helpless in the gladiator's grip, and he held her in front of him as a shield. "Dirdra has returned to me," he said in a voice cold with disdain. "Do not try to claim her again, for she is mine. You will return to your ship and bring her to Madura." Then he turned Dirdra roughly to face him. "You have returned freely—so I will be kind. Kwinn is waiting for you, Dirdra. He lives . . . and longs for his sister."

Astra was Reading full out now. Torio and Melissa joined minds with her, recognizing what terrified her so.

The man before them, holding them at bay with his sword and squeezing Dirdra's arm so hard that at any moment it might break, had the appearance of the man who had journeyed with them all the way from Zendi.

But Astra knew—and the other Readers knew with her: it was not Zanos!

Chapter Four

All knew at once that it was Maldek who spoke through Zanos. The gladiator's open, friendly features took on the cold disdain they had seen in Dirdra's memory—but even as with one mind the Readers searched for a way to get Dirdra away from Zanos and subdue him without hurting him, they Read Zanos himself fighting for control.

Roaring like a wounded bear, he threw Dirdra from him and raised his sword—but there was nothing to strike at. "No man controls me against my will!" the gladiator exclaimed. Astra's mind at once joined her husband's to reject the Master Sorcerer's influence.

Maldek was, of course, out of body, but he could project to the Readers. Melissa knelt beside Dirdra, Reading that her arm was badly bruised, but not broken. Then she became unReadable for a moment, as she focused healing power.

Torio, meanwhile, was wondering how far Maldek was from his body. It was somewhere on the island of Madura, obviously, across the strait separating that land from Brettonia. But the strait was narrow, if treacherous—less than a day's journey by ship. If Maldek was near the shore, he was traveling no farther out of body than Torio had often done.

//I have no need to impress you, boy,// Maldek answered his thought. //If you are skilled at the inner sight, you may be useful to me ... or at least amusing. Just what good do you think that sword will do you against powers such as mine?//

//I won't know until we meet,// Torio replied, and Melissa looked up at him, smiling encouragement.

And that brought Maldek's attention to Melissa. //Ahh ... a dark beauty, as lovely in her way as Dirdra. And with powers. My little Maduran minnow has lured quite a catch to my shores! Tell Dirdra I am pleased with the outcome of her adventure ... as I trust all of you will be when you come to me. For come you must, will you nill you, though the way be hard and dangerous. By the end of your journey each of you will find what you seek ... even if you do not now know what that is.//

With that, Maldek's presence was gone—but they were not alone. The seven men Torio had noticed earlier were running into the baths, past the bubbling warm pool and into the cavern with the waterfall.

Brandishing their tools as weapons, they demanded, "Leave our land!"

"You Madurans—nothing but trouble!"

"You'll bring the wrath of the Master Sorcerers down on us again!"

"Back to your ship—we'll not shield you here!"

Zanos, Astra, and Torio could easily have subdued the seven poorly armed workmen, but they could Read their memories of Maldek's search for Dirdra months ago—setting fire burning through people's nerves, killing their livestock, blinding and laming their children as he demanded news of a beautiful red-haired woman no one had seen . . . for with all Maldek's powers, he had not known that Dirdra had passed this way in the guise of a boy, and disappeared into the land of the Dark Forest before he knew she was out of Madura.

Rather than fight these poor people who had already suffered so much at Maldek's hands, the five hastily threw on their outer garments and let themselves be pushed out of the caverns. The last thing Melissa reached for was the garland of flowers Torio had made for her . . . but it was brown and withered as if it had been seared with frost.

Outside, the workers prodded them along the cliff path. "Go back to Madura!" said one of the men, shoving Melissa with his pikestaff. "Stay where you belong—don't bring your troubles on other folk!"

Torio pushed the man's staff aside. "She's not Maduran. She's a healer!"

Another man laughed bitterly. "We know Madurans now, if we didn't before! We send 'em all back—even the dark uns!"

And Torio Read that the man saw him as obviously Maduran, even though his hair was brown, not red. His eyes were a clear blue-green, revealed when one of the savage healers had removed his cataracts in the mistaken belief that that would cure his blindness.

I suppose I could pass for Maduran, he realized.

Dirdra remained silent, pale and tight-lipped, as they were herded to the ship. The crew were also being driven aboard, protesting all the way.

The captain was waiting for them. "If the sorcerers want you," he told them, "let them come and get you! I'll not risk Madura now!"

"But you've been paid—" Zanos began.

"We'll take you just as far," the captain replied, "up north to Hrothsland. That's a great seafaring nation—someone from there will be foolhardy enough to take you to Madura."

"But we made an agreement," Zanos protested.

Astra put her hand on his arm. //Let it go for now. No one's been hurt. The captain will change his mind once we're out to sea.//

But it was the sea that changed.

From calm swells, it developed into choppy waves that carried them inexorably westward—toward Madura.

The captain adjusted the sails and tried to steer northward, but the wind grew stronger . . . and colder.

Torio knew what was happening. He had been the Reader guiding Wulfston and Rolf when they had raised the storm to halt the attacking Aventine fleet. Melissa was a survivor of one of the resulting shipwrecks.

They wrapped up in woolen cloaks and stood at the rail, Reading as far as they could toward Madura—but it was beyond the range of any Reader aboard, unless one of them risked going out of body in the dangerously heaving ship.

No one had to do that to know that Maldek was causing the storm. The captain was forced to sub-

mit, or lose his ship. Grimly, he ordered the helms-
man to take a westward course. At once the sails
billowed with a fresh breeze as, against the prevailing winds, the ship was carried toward Madura.

Once they had accepted the course Maldek
wanted them to take, Torio expected the Adept
influence to stop. But the breeze continued. "How
long can he keep that up?" he wondered aloud.

"Maldek is not using his energy now," Dirdra
said in a hollow voice. "He controls hundreds of
people with smaller powers. Some of his weather
talents will drive themselves into collapse this night.
Maldek won't."

She turned to her four companions, her face lit
harshly by the late-afternoon sun. "I am so sorry.
I did not think Maldek would even remember
me—just another of the many he has used as his
toys."

"I understand the type," said Zanos. "You escaped him—and that is something he cannot stand."

"Yes. I knew he would take his revenge if I
succeeded in freeing Kwinn—but I thought that
by returning with a group of strangers I might
reach Maldek's castle unnoticed. Instead, I have
brought Maldek's attention to you—and you will
suffer for my stupidity."

"Dirdra, we came of our own free will," Melissa
pointed out. "Surely four people with both Reading and Adept powers would not long have escaped the notice of the Master Sorcerers. As it is,
one of them is aiding us in reaching Madura."

"The most powerful . . . and the most evil," said
Dirdra.

Remembering that Dirdra did not know what
Maldek had told the Readers after Zanos had

shaken off his possession, Torio said, "Maldek said the way would be hard and dangerous."

"He is playing games with you already!" Dirdra replied. "Now he knows I am within the range of his powers, he will toy with us as a cat does with a field mouse before the kill. If he wanted us directly, he would have the ship sail up the river to his castle. We could be there by noon tomorrow."

But the wind drove the ship south as well as west, all through the short night of early summer, and in the gray dawn light they anchored along an empty shore, bleak and uninhabited.

The five adventurers went ashore in a small boat—and by the time they had beached it, the ship was already well out to sea.

The morning was rainy and chill. They wore clothes suitable for an Aventine winter, and shivered as the cold penetrated.

"Which way?" asked Zanos as they slogged through mud up to a trail which followed a ridge overlooking the sea.

Torio Read east and west along the trail. "There's an abandoned settlement about a mile to the east," he reported. "We can shelter there long enough to dry out our clothes."

"Torio's right," said Melissa. "None of us have enough Adept strength to use it for hours on end just to keep warm, dry, and healthy."

"Not and be awake when we're really needed!" Astra put in with a forced smile.

They were all starting out tired, as no one had thought of sleeping last night. They had eaten just before dawn—ship's rations, though, for the aborted stop in Brettonia had not resulted in the intended acquisition of supplies. Thus only Zanos, whose combination of athlete's and Adept's metabolism made him perpetually hungry, had eaten much.

Tumbled walls and roofless buildings greeted them in what once must have been a fishing village. Remnants of the stone supports for a pier still marched across the beach and disappeared into the water. Gulls as gray as the sea and sky called harshly and hungrily as they skimmed over the deserted sand.

"This is not how I remember home!" protested Zanos. "At this time of year it should be warm— there should be flowers blooming in the gardens, roses climbing the walls. My village was laid out just like this—it has to be along this coast somewhere. But it was bright and cheerful . . . and alive!"

Only wisps of dry weeds blew in the sea wind. Torio knew Zanos was right—if the climate were as he described, wildflowers would bloom here as they did in Brettonia. Not even dead remains of rose vines clung to the walls; it had been cold and bleak here for a long time.

One building had a wooden roof, warped and gray with weathering, but offering the most shelter in the area. They built a fire with what few scraps of wood they could find, only Zanos' Adept power able to get it started, and huddled around it to warm their hands and faces.

With the blankets from their bedrolls hung across the empty windows and doorway, they were able to get the one-room cottage warm enough to strip the boots and stockings off their freezing feet. Leaving their clothes to steam-dry, they toasted their toes and drank the herb tea Melissa made, feeling somewhat better.

Knowing that it was likely they would have to make part of their journey afoot, they had all packed money, as Decius had advised Torio. Now, though, having to use their bedding to keep the chill wind out of the cottage, they were left with nothing to wrap up in except dry undergarments, and each other.

Torio hefted the sack of gold coins he had brought. "It's all very fine to plan to buy what we need—but where? I haven't Read another human being since we came ashore. Have you, Astra, Melissa?" he asked the other Magister Readers.

"No one," the women agreed.

"We don't even know which way to go," said Zanos, taking his maps out of their waterproof case and unrolling them on the stone floor. "Where are we?"

"Somewhere along this southern stretch," Torio replied, running his finger along what on the map was many miles of shore. "Let me go out of body, and I'll give you an accurate Reading."

The stone floor was cold to stretch out on—but Zanos concentrated on him, and Torio felt his body warmth stop dissipating into the ground. He smiled a thank-you to the gladiator, then composed himself and let his "self" drift upward.

When one escaped discomfort, it was always a sore temptation to remain out of body. No rain or cold assaulted him now, and he felt light and free as he followed the trail eastward—for the map showed far more settlements in that direction, suggesting a greater chance that some of them had survived.

Sure enough, where a main road met the trail they were on, there was a decent-sized town with an inn and a stable. They would have to walk all day to get there, but the knowledge that they could sleep in dry, warm beds and buy warm clothes and horses for the rest of their journey would make the trek more bearable.

Remembering the map, Torio followed the main road northward to where Maldek's castle sat on the edge of a navigable river—the one Dirdra had said would have been the short route to reach the Master Sorcerer. Not knowing how sensitive a Reader he might be, Torio did not attempt to locate Maldek within the castle, but noted that it was protected by moats on three sides and the river on the other. A thriving city stood near the castle, with ships on the river loading and unloading trade goods. So not all of Madura was as desolate as this area where they had landed.

There was only one bridge across the river, leading to the main north-south road Torio was following. It entered the city several miles from the castle, which stood on the north bank to the east of the city, with a small strip of forest between.

There was a denser forest, though, on the north-south road between the southern coast and the city. That, Torio guessed, was where lay the dangers that Maldek had promised. Even without lingering to examine closely, he Read both bears and wolves in the wood—hungry animals looking to feed their young.

What was missing from the picture was agriculture. Only a few of the cleared fields between the forest and the shore were cultivated. Most lay fallow, deserted, young trees beginning to encroach on their edges. There were a few swine and cows, and more sheep, but they were not thriving. There was not enough production here to feed the people of that city.

Maldek had to be either trading for food or letting his people go hungry. With even his limited knowledge of ruling a land, Torio knew that the former was merely a slower way of destroying the country than the latter. Yet power-mad rulers often took farmers away from the job of feeding their people to fight wars or be otherwise used at the lord's pleasure. Eventually, it would lead to Maldek's downfall, as just such neglect of his people had led to Drakonius'.

However, the five adventurers didn't have time to wait for Maldek's government to collapse. They had to reach Maldek's castle, rescue Dirdra's brother . . . and in the process try to find out about the sorcerers who might rule other Maduran lands. It was obvious already that Maldek was not the healer Melissa sought. Even if he *could* restore injured people to wholeness or return life to the slain, clearly he would not teach anyone else except at an unacceptable price.

But perhaps the Madura Zanos remembered flourished somewhere else in these islands. Torio certainly hoped so.

He returned to his body and told the others what he had found—but as he turned to show them on the map exactly where they were, he put his finger right on the place worn thin by Zanos' own finger as he had made his plans to return . . . home.

The gladiator stiffened when he realized that this desolate deserted village was indeed the place

where he had lived as a child, until the day slavers
had raided it and carried him off to Tiberium.

Astra, Reading her husband's feelings, reached
out to empathize—only to waken his memories of
that terrible day when the slavers had come.

The ship anchored offshore, and a boatload of
men rowed to land—nothing unusual about that.
Ships often arrived along this coast, looking to
trade or to recruit strong young men for their
crews.

Young Zanos sat on the pier, sunburned, hands
blistered from the net he was trying to repair with
as yet unskilled hands. He'd rather have been out
with the fishing fleet, but his father insisted that
he wait until he was ten—"Then maybe ye'll get
some strength to ye, lad!"

The first of today's small fishing vessels were
back already, and the air was redolent with the
smell as women cleaned the fish that would become tonight's supper all through the village, throwing the refuse off the pier for the gulls.

The strangers, it seemed, were looking for a
tavern. The village had only old Walvo's, where
jugs of mead or ale were sold to be carried home.
The newcomers insisted that would be fine—"We've
got a great thirst on us," said their leader, whose
sunburst tattoo attracted Zanos' immediate attention.

Maybe one day he would leave this small village
and see the world. Maybe he would wear a tattoo
like that one—which he saw on other arms and
realized marked every member of the ship's crew.
Many wore gold hoop earrings, too—and one man's
grin displayed a golden tooth!

As the scouts waved the others ashore, Zanos

left his work and tagged along in wide-eyed delight, only to lose the strangers' attention to the village girls until their mothers called them in to help with supper. Then the sailors, who could not possibly have all crowded into Walvo's, sat on the sandy beach and played games with dice, or with throwing knives.

In the hubbub, Zanos found it easy to pretend he couldn't hear his mother calling him as he mingled with the strangers, finding the ones who spoke some Maduran, begging for stories of far-off lands.

As the tide came in, so did the rest of the fishing fleet. The village men were none too happy to find their wives cooking extra food for strangers who had brought pins, scissors, and small, sharp paring knives—or their sons and daughters hanging on the sailors' every word.

But the sailors bought a round of ale for everyone, and handed out glass and cork floats for the fishnets—and soon what had started as an ordinary day turned into one big party.

Zanos' older brother, Bryen, had been out with the fishing fleet—he had just turned eleven, and had gone out with their father for a year now. Zanos' had envied him—until today, when Bryen had missed half the fun.

But now Bryen came to spoil Zanos' fun. "Mother needs you to do your chores, Zanos!" the older boy announced. "She needs kindling cut and water drawn—hurry up, now!"

All the household chores had fallen to Zanos once his brother started going out with the fleet, and he resented being the younger, smaller one, getting stuck ashore. *I'll show Bryen,* he thought.

*I'll sneak aboard that ship and sail away—and when I
come back I'll be as rich as those sailors, with gifts for
everybody!*

Muttering to himself, he set about his chores
with bad grace—but as he trudged from the well
with two heavy water buckets suspended from the
yoke across his shoulders, he heard a sudden commotion from the beach. Looking down toward it,
he saw that the ship had come in on the tide, and
was now anchored at the end of the pier—and in
the light of the flickering fires they had built on
the beach at sunset, people were milling about—

To his horror, Zanos saw two sailors grab one of
the village men and stab him through the heart!

Others were reaching for the women, shoving
them toward the pier as they drew their weapons
and slew unarmed fishermen right and left.

Letting the water buckets fall, Zanos sped toward
his home, shouting, "Mother! Hwelda! Run— *run*!"

His mother and his sister came to the door of
their cottage to see what the commotion was.

"Run! Hurry!" Zanos cried as he ran up to them
and tried to grab their hands and pull them toward
the garden, where the smell of roses filled the air.

"Hwelda—go with Zanos!" their mother directed,
and started toward the beach.

"Mother—no!" cried Hwelda. She was fifteen,
stocky, and too strong for Zanos to hold. All he
could do was tag after the two women, begging
them to come back.

Then they saw Zanos' father and brother running toward them. "Go back!" shouted their father. "Up the hill and onto the moor! Hurry!"

But five sailors ran after them—Zanos' mother
screamed as she saw her husband struck down

from behind, brains and blood splashing across
her feet.

With a shrieking wail, she fell to her knees beside her husband—and the same sailor stabbed
her in the back. She slumped across her husband's
body.

Hwelda screamed, and began to keen in the way
of the village women at the death of one of their
family. Zanos stood frozen in disbelief—this could
not be happening!

Bryen somehow came to his senses. "Hwelda—
come on!" he cried. "Zanos—help me!"

Bryen grasped his sister's hand on one side,
Zanos on the other—but the five sailors caught
the three children easily. "Let go, damn you!"
growled one with a blond beard, trying to shake
Bryen's grip off Hwelda's arm. "Let me see what
I've caught!"

"No! Let my sister alone!" shouted Bryen.

"Let her alone!" Zanos echoed, taking courage
from his brother.

The sailors laughed, and one shoved Zanos aside,
another grabbing his arms as he tried to reach for
Hwelda's hand again. He squirmed and kicked,
but aroused only laughter in his captor. "This
one's got spirit," said the sailor. "With that red
hair and hot temper, he'll bring a good price in
Tiberium!"

Bryen was still trying to haul Hwelda away—
and for a moment succeeded in dragging the
trembling girl loose from the grip of her captors.
"That's enough!" said one of them—and with his
sword he slashed off Bryen's hand.

The hand still clung to Hwelda's wrist as she
shrieked again. Bryen made no sound, but fell to

his knees, eyes wide in disbelief as he instinctively
clasped his good hand around his mutilated wrist.

"You've ruined a good laborer, damn you, Shoff!"
exclaimed the blond-bearded one. Then he turned
Hwelda toward the light, and cursed roundly. "This
one's fat and freckled—the boy'd have brought
three times as much! No use taking any but pretty
women in the space we've got!" And he grabbed
Hwelda's hair, tilted her head back, and slit her
throat.

"We'll take that one," he added, pointing at
Zanos—and the boy found himself being picked
up bodily and carried toward the pier.

"No!" he shouted, kicking as hard as he could.

The blond one paid no attention as he turned
with his knife to dispatch Bryen—but over his
captor's shoulder Zanos saw that his brother was
gone.

"Should I go after him?" asked one of the other
men.

"Nah—he's no good now. He'll bleed to death
anyhow. Come on—let's get down there and see if
we can catch us a *good* woman!"

Zanos' memory came to an abrupt halt, as his
eyes traveled about the circle of his friends and he
realized that all the Readers had experienced it
with him.

Then he stood, grabbed up his half-dry woolen
cloak, and stalked out of the cottage.

"Zanos—" Torio began.

"Let him go," said Astra. "He has dreamed of
coming back for so long, and finding his home
still here, his brother still alive. Now he must come
to terms with the reality."

"Maldek did it on purpose!" Dirdra said angrily,

the only one who had not experienced the vision. "He must have Read what Zanos was searching for—and he brought us right here, just to hurt him!"

"He said we would each find what we came looking for," said Melissa. "At least Zanos came with the knowledge that' it was possible he would find his home exactly like this."

But some time later, leaving the women to get ready for their journey, Torio went out to find Zanos.

The gladiator sat huddled in his cloak, on one of the mounds of stone on the beach. He was unReadable, using his Adept powers to keep warm. Wordlessly, Torio handed him leggings and boots.

Under that gray sky, even Zanos' fire-red hair seemed faded. The drizzling rain obscured the cottages from the beach. Torio stopped visualizing, wondering how nonReaders coped by sight alone on such days—it was less depressing, too, merely to Read where he was going by the "feel" of it, without having to see the bleakness of the seascape.

Even the waves pounding the shore sounded desolate in Torio's ears. Zanos, though, had recovered some of his optimism. "I knew it might be like this," he said. "Just because no one's living here anymore, that doesn't mean my brother isn't living somewhere else. I didn't see him die—he had the strength to run away from the slavers. Men have recovered from such wounds. Since our home is gone, it will simply be harder to find him, that's all."

And Torio felt the sea wind whip through his cloak again as the roar of the waves sounded for a moment more like the rumbling of doom, bearing down upon them in their helpless darkness. Yet . . . "When you find your brother," he said, "he will have his hand again."

Zanos stared at him. "Is that—?"

"Yes. I don't know how I know it, and I don't know any more than what I just told you . . . but you will find your brother."

The gladiator managed a small smile. "Thank you, Torio . . . even though I somehow knew that much myself."

But then Melissa called, "Torio! Zanos! We're ready!" and the two men joined the three women for the long, weary journey to the town Torio had found.

Everything went amazingly as planned. Although they were all weary when they arrived—especially the three with Adept powers, who had shored everyone up along the way—there were actually rooms at the inn, and Torio and Dirdra were able to haggle down the price of horses so that all could ride in the morning.

After a good meal, they retired to their rooms just as most people were arriving at the inn. Dirdra took the first watch—on the assumption that if anyone planned to attack them, it would be later, when it was more likely for travelers to be asleep. After four hours, she woke Torio, for the Adepts were the ones who needed to restore their energies.

He Read all secure—suspiciously so. Had Maldek forgotten them? Been distracted by something else? Or was it part of his game to give them this time to recover? Possibly he had some notion of fair play, or simply lost interest if his opposition were too easy to defeat. Torio longed to go out of body to spy on Maldek, but dared not do so without someone guarding his body. So he Read as far as he could, and waited.

Whatever the reason, absolutely nothing happened that night, and in the morning the travelers ate a hearty breakfast and set off on the road north to the capital city.

It was a two-day ride—and Torio could Read no place to break their journey except within the forest. Although there were many people on the road when they left the seacoast town, the farther north they traveled the fewer people they saw, and the worse the road became.

They had bought some more layers of warm clothing before leaving town, and today the sun shone, although the breeze was brisk. Once they were a few miles away from the sea wind, they were actually comfortable on their ride. Everyone cheered up.

Until they entered the forest. It loomed abruptly, like a wall across the road ahead—although once they got there they could see the road disappearing into it. Huge trees cut off the sun, and met above the roadway—which in many places was overgrown to a narrow path where they had to ride single-file. Dense undergrowth spread in every direction, and beneath the canopy of trees the sunny day became dim as twilight.

The Readers kept a watch for dangers, and for the proper trail, for there were often forks and byways. Off in the woods, a few deer fled at the sound of their passage, but wolves and bears sniffed the air and listened, deciding whether they were hungry enough to risk attacking.

Although he Read no people in the forest, Torio

was reminded powerfully of a journey he had made with Wulfston over a year ago, when the roads between Zendi and Wulfston's lands were not yet free of bandits. Noticing Dirdra shivering, not with cold but with apprehension, he said, "Don't worry—you're with Readers and Adepts. We can handle wild animals, or anything else that comes along." And, to pass the weary miles, he began to tell of the adventure he had had that day with Wulfston.

As he and Wulfston rode through the glorious spring afternoon, Torio Read carefully ahead. Nothing difficult lay before them; the streams had calmed from their recent torrents, and they could relax and enjoy a pleasant ride.

Suddenly, though, something out of the ordinary impinged on Torio's contentment. "Wulfston—there's a band of men waiting in that wood ahead of us."

"Can you Read anything about them? Fear? Anger?"

"Some of both. They haven't seen us yet . . . but we're what they're waiting for. It's an ambush!"

"Foolish!" said Wulfston. "You'd think they'd know by now that with a Reader to guide him, a Lord Adept is practically invulnerable. Do you recognize anyone?"

"No—not your people. Hill bandits, from their dress. They might be waiting to try to take any travelers who come along."

"They probably don't know you're a Reader, even if they've recognized me." The black Adept knew well how conspicuous he was. "Are they on both sides of the road?"

"Yes." Torio explained how far ahead their would-be attackers were, and watched as Wulfston concentrated.

Torio didn't know what the Adept would do. He must find a way to work with nature, not waste his strength working against her, for they had spent the morning aiding flatlands villagers to dig a well to water their fields in the dry season, Torio guiding and Wulfston using his Adept power to break through rock layers and hold back the debris so that the villagers could shovel it out without hindrance. The Adept had used considerable power, but had taken only a meal and a short rest before they started for home.

Torio feared Wulfston would use fire against their ambushers—it was one of the first powers he had learned to use as a child, and once started, it would take on a life of its own.

But the woods were full of new growth, baby animals—

Before Torio could draw breath to protest against fire, he Read that Wulfston had called upon a different power. On one side of the road, a mother bear stood up and sniffed the air, scenting the gathered bandits as danger to her cubs. She began lumbering in their direction as on the other side a pair of wolves herded their young into their den and set off at a lope toward the second group of hiding men.

Ordinarily, both bear and wolves would have ignored the men near the road, for the animals were not hungry and the men had made no actual move toward their cubs. But under Wulfston's strange power to "call" animals, they moved swiftly through the underbrush.

Wulfston urged his horse forward, Torio following.

The bear broke through the brush behind the first group and rose to her full height with a growl. Horses shied and men panicked, dashing for the road as across from them the pair of wolves raced between the legs of the other gang's horses, nipping and snarling.

Both groups of bandits swarmed onto the road, running into each other as Wulfston and Torio converged upon them. The Adept raised his hand, and a thunderbolt roared toward the terrified men, missing the nearest of them by a handspan.

All three wild animals, released from Wulfston's hypnotic power, turned tail and ran back into the woods at the flash and noise, but the bandits fled along the road, Wulfston and Torio now in pursuit.

"We didn't have to chase them far," Torio finished, noting with satisfaction that his audience were all grinning at the image of the fleeing bandits. "I'm sure they're still spinning tall tales of the day they had the bad judgment to ambush a Lord Adept—although we never saw them again."

"I wish I'd been there," said Melissa. "I've never seen Lord Wulfston use that ability—but Torio, don't you agree that it has to be related to Reading? How does he know there are any animals out there to call?"

"I don't know," Torio replied. "All I know is that it works—but nothing any of us have done can get Wulfston to learn to Read, any more than I can learn Adept tricks."

"You will," said Zanos. "It's all the same—"

Suddenly, without warning, the wind rose, howling into cyclone force right there in the middle of the forest. Trees whipped, birds screamed, and the five travelers had to fight their terrified horses. Ahead of them, huge trees were ripped up by the roots—and fell right across the path they had to take.

It was over as fast as it had come, the wind dropping to nothing, forest debris floating down through the dappled light, the birds and animals still silent in their fear.

With one mind, the Readers Read outward to their limits—but they could find no sign of Maldek or anyone else spying on them. Then they turned to the trees in their path—four of them, tangled into a pile that thoroughly blocked their way forward.

"This is only the beginning," said Zanos. "We don't have the physical strength to shove them aside. Is there a way around?"

The better Readers only confirmed what the gladiator already knew: there was not.

"Then it's fire," said Zanos. "I'll start it. Astra, Melissa—you confine it, so it just gives us a path. I'll have to concentrate on keeping it small. We don't want to start a forest fire."

Torio was accustomed to Wulfston's Adept strength; this situation would hardly have been a challenge to him. But Zanos' powers were small compared to Wulfston's; he coaxed a small flame to begin among the dry leaves, then guided it along a branch to the trunk. It was slow work, as they dared not let it leap into flames which might be beyond the powers of the three with Adept ability to control.

It took almost an hour, first to guide the fire,

then to Read for every spark and make certain it
was completely out before they could ride their
horses over the ashes now paving the trail.

And no sooner were they beyond that wearying
task than Torio Read a pack of wolves slinking up
on them, fearful but hungry.

This trial was easier. Astra said, "I'll scare them
off," and reached for the animals' minds with
hers. It was a technique neither Torio nor Melissa
had studied, but they knew it was the way Readers
treated sick minds, combined with Adept powers.
Astra let herself Read the wolves' simple thoughts
and desires, then somehow, becoming unReadable, twisted them so that instead of five people
and five horses—potential food—the wolves saw
five huge, angry bears. Saw them, smelled them—
and turned tail and ran.

But as Torio was about to congratulate Astra on
ridding them of that nuisance with so little use of
power, he realized that while he had been concentrating on what she was doing he had neglected to
notice something else—there were people coming
toward them through the woods.

"Melissa—Read!" he exclaimed, for she, too, had
been fascinated with Astra's trick, which presum-
ably she could duplicate.

In every direction that they Read, they found
people. People? There were flesh-and-blood human bodies moving toward them, breathing, hearts
beating—but there seemed to be no minds within
them to Read!

All Adepts braced to use their powers? So many?
Then it was hopeless, for there must be fifty of
them moving purposefully toward them through

the dense underbrush, ignoring scratches and bruises, stumbling and picking themselves up—

They moved like no Adepts Torio had ever known. They were more like puppets—like the two people they had seen in Dirdra's memory.

But these were not the beautiful young people of that scene in Maldek's castle. These were repulsive creatures, dressed in rags, skin peeling off, missing fingers or toes, eyelids gone to reveal staring eyes—

It seemed an army of the dead!

"Orbu!" gasped Dirdra as the first of them came into sight through the brush.

"They're mindless—but they *are* alive!" said Melissa. And as one of them raised a spear as if to heave it at her, she neatly stopped the creature's heart. It dropped, truly dead.

As if that were the signal, the rest increased their pace, converging on the five travelers, giving off the stench of rotting flesh.

Torio and Zanos drew their swords, lopping off heads as the mindless beings made no attempt to defend themselves, but pressed forward with knives and spears, attempting to reach their prey, trampling the bodies of the fallen as they came.

And behind them another wave of orbu followed, equally mindless although physically in somewhat better condition, as if Maldek had first sent the most defective ones, the most expendable.

Wave after wave of them surged through the woods, enveloping the five companions in their sheer numbers. Torio could not count how many he killed before one reached him with a knife and gashed his thigh. Too late, he cut the thing's arm off as another pulled him off his horse and stabbed him in his left biceps.

Wherever he sliced at one, another came from a different direction, slashing at him without aim other than to draw blood. Around him, the others fought equally hard, Dirdra kicking them away, stabbing them with a spear she had picked up from one of them, until finally she, too, disappeared under a mass of bodies.

The latecomers were sturdier—heads and limbs were harder to cut off, and Torio's strength was giving out. This was not the fighting he was trained in—there was no art here. Zanos grabbed one of the creatures and used it to knock down half a dozen others—but they felt no pain, and were up again at once, charging at him. He looked at one and stopped its heart, but three others caught him from behind, and he went down under their weight.

Torio Read a knife slip between Zanos' ribs and slice through the vessels in his lung—a death blow if he were not healed almost at once! "Astra!" he shouted—but Zanos' wife was waging her own private war against the loathsome creatures, swinging a short sword in either hand as he had seen her practicing with Zanos aboard ship.

Torio drove his sword through the heart of another orbu, grabbed the spear it dropped, turned, and lunged at two of them, skewering both on the same spear with their own momentum. The things seemed even more agitated, more determined.

And daring to focus beyond his immediate vicinity, he realized—"Maldek's run out of them! These are the last!"

His cry gave heart to the other fighters. Slip-

ping on blood and flesh, Torio dispatched the last
three in the group attacking him, Read Dirdra
fling her way out from under the bodies piled on
her, Melissa, the only one still on her horse, stop
the hearts of two more, and Astra slash the throats
of her three final attackers.

Only Zanos did not move. He was unconscious,
under a heap of dead orbu.

Frantically, the other four dug Zanos out. Together, Astra and Melissa stopped his bleeding
and closed the wound, but they were exhausted.
None of the Adepts could perform further until
they had rested—but not here, amid the gore of
battle.

Limping, Torio helped Dirdra round up the
horses. It took the strength of Torio and all three
women to heave Zanos across his saddle. Astra
and Melissa were fighting sleep, and the use of
Adept powers had reduced their Reading ability
to that of children. Torio was their only lookout,
and he could feel the stinging of his wounds now,
Read the infection from the filthy implements with
which he had been cut.

Blinking, Melissa swayed as she faced him. "Torio
. . . I have to heal you—no choice." She touched
his shoulder, and the heat of Adept healing
cleansed the wound. Then his thigh—a deep
wound, and painful. He winced as the heat increased the pain, but knew she dared not put him
to sleep. He would have to stand it somehow, until
they got to where it was safe for him to let go
consciousness.

And where was that? Melissa leaned on him.
"Can't sleep," she murmured, although he could
feel how hard she had to fight it.

"Get on your horse," he said. "I'll lead you."

Astra was half asleep, leaning against Zanos as she sent her husband from unconsciousness into the healing sleep. Dirdra guided her to her horse and helped her into the saddle, then mounted her own horse, holding Astra's reins.

Torio led both Zanos and Melissa. It was slow going, but already hungry predators were converging on the scene of battle. At least if they were busy gorging themselves there, they would not be available to attack the helpless travelers.

The path was as rough as ever, and as the sun slanted westward the horses stumbled. When Torio Read a rocky outcropping ahead that formed almost a shallow cave, he decided it was time to stop. He could Read no trace of Maldek, but of course if the Master Sorcerer were simply watching them out of body, not trying to Read their thoughts, he could not be Read unless he wanted to be—or unless he slipped up and projected his presence unintentionally.

Besides, Maldek had said he wanted them to come to him. And he had not used his Adept powers to strike them down now that they were virtually helpless. Sharp waves of pain went through Torio's thigh with every step of his horse, and the healing heat only increased it. Still, he knew that if he lay down, he would fall asleep despite the pain. It would leave them without a lookout, for Astra was in no better shape than Melissa. But they had to stop somewhere.

Dared he assume that Maldek would find no pleasure in slaughtering them in their sleep?

"I'll stand watch, Torio," said Dirdra when they came to a halt at the obvious campsite.

"You're not a Reader."

"And how much of a Reader are you when you're injured and exhausted? Just help me get the others settled, and then you sleep. I'll build a fire to keep the animals away. I doubt there'll be any people stirring in *this* wood by night. And," she echoed his thought, "if Maldek meant to take us while we cannot fight back, he would surely have done so by now."

Torio was simply too tired to protest. He sagged into his bedroll and was asleep without another thought.

Torio woke to some sound that had stopped by the time he dragged himself fully conscious. The moment he Read where he was, he remembered—and without moving assessed his situation.

It was just before dawn—but in these northern climes the sun rose early in the summer. Summer? There was frost on the ground—even on the blankets covering the travelers!

No one else was awake. Zanos was in healing sleep, Melissa and Astra equally deep in the dreamless sleep of recovery from the use of Adept powers. Dirdra sat with her back against the stone outcropping, spear at her side, but she was in that same deep sleep bordering on coma. NonReader, nonAdept, she had not entered that state by herself.

The sound that had wakened Torio came again—a growl. A very deep, threatening growl.

He Read its source sniffing around the outskirts of their camp, attracted by the stench of blood and gore from the battle they had waged against the orbu. Torio felt half sick from the putrid stink of his own splattered clothing.

The animal attracted by the stench was a wolf.
No—a dog. A dog bigger than a wolf, easily out-
weighing Torio, but lean, built like a racing hound
and covered in shaggy gray hair. It was all muscle,
sinew, and teeth—and it was hungry.

The beast sniffed again, smelling the death smell
of the splattered gore and the life smell of the
five travelers. Its stomach rumbled, and it moved
toward Dirdra, prepared to kill and eat.

"No!" ordered Torio, sitting up. "Get back!"

The animal turned, hackles rising, and bared its
teeth at him with a threatening growl.

How he longed for Wulfston's gift of controlling animals!

But if it was a form of Reading, then—

He Read the animal—the stench increasing in
his nostrils with the dog's sensitive nose, but becoming attractive, increasing the hunger, the hunting instinct.

But there was another instinct in the animal. It
was dog, not wolf—it had once been accustomed
to obeying man, until its master had died and it
had gone wild to survive.

Hunger drove it now—and hatred of men who
had driven it off with pitchforks and clubs when it
had gone after sheep or chickens. It sought ven-
geance for the many blows it had received, food
stolen right out of its mouth.

The dog growled again, slavering, lips pulled
back completely, the hair on its back standing
straight up as it faced Torio, stiff-legged, assessing
him as prey. Helpless prey in the dark—to his
astonishment, Torio Read that the animal sensed
he was blind.

Where was his sword? In its scabbard, under

the blankets—he'd been so exhausted he'd fallen asleep wearing it. He'd never get it out and untangled from his bedroll before the animal tore his throat out.

He Read the dog catch a whiff of his startlement and crouch to spring.

//No!// he projected instinctively, as if to a child who had just begun to Read. //No—you don't want to hurt me. You want someone to care for you—to feed you.//

The animal stopped in confusion, growling again but not attacking.

There was food in the packs somewhere—supplies they had bought in town. Torio projected an image: the dog sitting before him, Torio stroking him and giving—giving *him*; the animal was male—a piece of cheese. He projected intense pleasure, security, love.

The dog sat down, sniffing the air in confusion.

Again Torio projected the image. The dog whined.

Holding his breath, Torio pulled his legs up and slid out of his bedroll, moving very slowly as he found his supplies where Dirdra had placed his saddlebags under his head as a pillow. He pulled out his food packet and unwrapped a chunk of cheese, broke off a piece, and held it out toward the dog.

Again projecting the image of petting and feeding the dog, Torio offered the tidbit, saying, "Here, boy. Come on. No one's going to hurt you."

He held his breath as the animal sniffed his outstretched hand—and then took the cheese. The dog sat back, waiting, and Torio broke off another piece and fed it again. There was nowhere near enough to satisfy the animal's appetite—but his need for human companionship was almost as strong. When the cheese was gone, he accepted bread until the desperate ache in his gut was appeased.

And then he butted his huge head against Torio's hand, as if demanding the petting he had promised!

He stroked the dog's head uncertainly—there had been no dogs at the Academy, just a cat that spent most of its time lounging before the fire in the kitchen. Wulfston had dogs, but Torio had never paid much attention to them.

But he quickly Read where the beast felt the most pleasure, scratching behind his ears, the sides of his face.

After a time, the beast got up and turned in a circle—then flopped down next to Torio, pressed his great body against Torio's, and fell asleep.

Dawn was breaking, but although they had fallen asleep before sunset, Zanos, Astra, and Melissa were still deeply asleep. Now that his charge of adrenaline from being awakened by the dog was gone, Torio was sleepy again. The warmth of the animal was comforting.

He thought of waking Dirdra, but suspected that the dog was a much better guardian than she could be. And something told him that a rapport had formed—from this point on, the great gray dog was his.

Sometime later, though, Torio woke alone. The sun was high in the sky. His companions were asleep—unharmed. For a moment Torio wondered if the incident with the animal had been a dream— but no, there was the empty napkin that had wrapped his cheese, and half his bread was gone as well. Furthermore, his blankets now sported a coating of wiry gray hairs.

He Read out beyond their camp, and found no sign of people. The dog was almost a mile away, following some kind of trail.

Torio turned his attention to his companions. Melissa woke when he Read her, and got up, stretching and yawning. She curled her lip. "Auf! I stink! We all do—and there's no place to wash."

"Sorry—this was the best camp I could find last night," said Torio.

"I'm not complaining," she replied. "I certainly was no help. You and Dirdra did very well, considering."

At the mention of her name, Dirdra woke, all apologies for having fallen asleep without waking Torio first. "We could have been murdered in our beds!"

"Eaten alive, rather," Torio told her.

"What?"

"You'll see—I think."

He was right. Melissa examined Torio's wounds, which, although only partly healed, had stopped hurting. Astra wakened and decided to wake Zanos to feed him, touching him on the forehead between the eyes—the only safe way to wake an Adept. By the time the gladiator had shaken off his drowsiness, the dog returned.

He brought back a rabbit, laid it at Torio's feet, and sat grinning at him proudly, tongue lolling out one side of his giant mouth.

The other four travelers stared as Torio patted the animal on the head. "I hate to tell you this, boy, but Readers are vegetarians."

"Adepts aren't!" said Zanos. "Where'd you get that creature, Torio?"

"He came in the middle of the night, and decided to adopt me," Torio replied, taking the rabbit and handing it to the gladiator. "I think we'd better share this with him, though." And as they built a fire to cook the rabbit and make tea, he told what had happened.

"It was Maldek again," said Dirdra. "I was too upset to sleep—but he must have made me. And then sent this beast to murder us."

"Don't blame the dog," said Torio. "He's just a poor stray that's been trying to survive since his master died. Look how he responded to a little bread and cheese."

"Fine animal," agreed Zanos. "They choose people, you know. People think they choose the dogs, but it's not so. The dog trainer at the arena used to tell me that only when the dog chose the man would they make a good team in the ring. You know how—? No, of course you never went to the games. But sometimes you'd swear man and dog were Reading one another."

Torio grinned. "This one's a Reader, all right—that's how I got through to him this morning."

"Really?" asked Melissa. //Here, boy!// she projected, as Torio had done.

But the huge dog didn't stir, just sat staring at Torio. Out of curiosity, he projected, //Go ahead,// and the image of Melissa petting the animal. At once the dog got up and walked over to Melissa, and let her scratch his shaggy head.

But he would take his orders only from Torio. Even when Zanos offered him the rabbit's entrails, he looked to Torio for permission before accepting food from anyone else. "He's chosen you, all right," said Zanos. "Now you'll have to name him."

"He probably has a name," said Torio. "What's your name, boy? What did your master call you?"

The dog understood only that Torio was asking something of him—he didn't understand what. So he dropped to the ground, looking up at Torio from under his eyebrows. When that was not the answer, he sat up and offered a hoof-sized paw. Torio took it, and patted him on the head. "You're trying to please me—I understand. But I want to know what to call you."

The dog tilted his head to one side, listening intently, frustrated that he could not make out what his new master wanted.

So Torio tried projecting to the dog the image of a man calling to him—the dog too far away to see his master, but hearing—what? What did he hear that caused him to stop what he was doing and run to the man?

And all the Readers heard it plain as could be in the dog's mind: //Gray!//

Torio laughed. "Gray! Good boy, Gray!" The dog grinned in delight, and almost knocked Torio over as his tail wagged the whole rest of his body. "Your master wasn't very original, but he loved you, didn't he?"

Again Gray didn't understand, but this time he knew it didn't matter—he had found his person, and he was happy.

It was late morning by the time the travelers set out once more, wending their way through dense forest until nearly sunset. Gray loped alongside Torio's horse most of the way, sometimes running off to trail interesting scents, sometimes leaping ahead, but it was clear he would stay with his new master.

Although the Readers remained alert, there were no new trials. When they came to a small creek at midafternoon, despite the chill air they stripped off their gory outer garments and washed them as clean as they could—until one of their group dared waste Adept powers on such a trivial task, some of the stains would remain permanent. But at least the smell was washed away.

As long as they had stopped, they ate while their clothes dried, and Zanos, whose wound was still bothering him, napped.

"Dirdra," asked Melissa, "exactly what are orbu?"

"They were people once," the Maduran woman answered. "The sorcerers steal their souls, and make their bodies do their bidding."

Astra shivered. "That's exactly what they felt like!"

Dirdra looked down at the bread she had been eating, and set it aside. "Maldek has made thousands of them. When the peasants would not give him in tribute the food they needed to feed their children, he took one out of every family, made him orbu, and left him living with his family, working the fields—someone they loved there beside them every day, eating and drinking and resting, but . . . dead!"

"Mindless," Melissa agreed.

"He has ruined our land," said Dirdra. "The orbu live only for a year or two. The first ones he set on us yesterday—they would have been dead in a few weeks anyway. They feel no pain. They simply go on doing as the sorcerer directs until they drop—or until they are killed as we killed those who attacked us. But Maldek has made so many, now there are not enough living people to till the fields and pay his tribute. He . . . seems to have learned that lesson, or else he has so much treasure in his castle now that he thinks he needs no more. At least for the past year or two he has stopped demanding tribute in goods, and has stopped turning masses of people orbu.

"Now he uses it more as an individual threat—and he demands a different tribute." She raised her eyes, flashing green fire. "I was the tribute he demanded from our village. He has turned other women orbu to serve him, but I think he has tired of that now. He was determined that I serve him freely—but I would not! He is evil! And I have brought his evil down upon you, who have become my friends."

"He's holding your brother hostage," said Torio. "Dirdra, we consider you our friend, as well. We're going to do everything we can to help you set your brother free."

She shook her head. "It is no use. Maldek holds in thrall too many with powers. Everyone fears him, for his own powers are greater than those of any Master Sorcerer in memory. He will take you, and toy with you like some great black cat—and then he will devour you!"

The sun was setting when they reached the northern edge of the forest, only a few miles from the city. By mutual consent, they rode on, planning to stay in the city overnight, and find out what they could about Maldek's castle in the morning.

But as they clattered across the bridge into the

city, armed guards waited for them on the opposite shore.

The Readers knew it, of course—but they Read
that the men had orders simply to take them to
Maldek's castle. There was little use resisting.

"Maldek is honored by your visit," the officer in
charge of the troop informed them. "We are your
escort." No sinister intent could be Read beyond
his words—only curiosity as to who this ragtag
band of weary travelers might be, that had aroused
such interest in the Master Sorcerer.

They had to ride on for more than an hour to
reach the castle—but then it might have taken that
long to find accommodations in the city. The road
through the forest which separated the castle from
the city was broad and well cared for—no need to
thread their horses through a tangle of undergrowth here.

The drawbridge was down for them—but it was
pulled up behind them with a sinister rumble once
they were inside the courtyard. Torio noted that it
was manipulated with a huge chain, not ropes—no
sword slash could let *this* drawbridge fall, nor could
a minor Adept easily break or burn through that
chain. Maldek expected to hold in—or out—people
of both cleverness and power.

Servants came running out to the courtyard,
boys to take their horses, women in clean dresses
with fresh white aprons, and a majordomo who
announced, "Maldek bids you welcome, gracious
ladies and gentlemen. If it will please you to follow, his servants will take you where you may
refresh yourselves before he grants you an inter-
view."

One of the boys came toward Gray with a collar

and leash. The dog, who was leaning so tightly against Torio as almost to knock him over, growled menacingly, and the boy backed off.

Trusting the animal's instincts, Torio said, "He stays with me," and hoped the beast was house-broken.

"As you wish, sir," said the lad with a bow, and Gray followed Torio inside.

They were taken to baths that rivaled the great bathhouse at Zendi. While they soaked away grime and weariness in the warm pool, servants brought them fruit and wine, nuts and cheese. Then other servants washed them with sweet-smelling soap—even Gray, who, although he enjoyed splashing in the cold pool, submitted to the lathering only at Torio's insistence. In the process, of course, he shook soapsuds so far into the corners that Torio was sure people would be slipping on them for weeks to come.

Finally, they were dried with soft towels and wrapped in silken robes. "If you gentlemen will come this way," said the majordomo, "I believe we can find garments suitable for you. The women will take care of the ladies."

"No—" began Zanos.

"It's all right," his wife told him. //Zanos, they've let us keep our weapons—which can only mean Maldek knows how little use they would be if he chose to use his powers against us now. We are Readers—he knows we can find one another, no matter what he does.//

So Zanos, Torio, and Gray were taken to a room where the men had their hair and beards combed and trimmed, and even the dog was brushed until he looked twice his size. Then the two men were fitted with silken tunics, covered with fur-trimmed, embroidered velvet robes. Under them went silken hose and soft felt ankle boots—warm indoor attire against the chill of the stone castle.

When they finally met with the approval of the majordomo, they were led through huge arched hallways inlaid with marble, gold, and precious stones, into a chamber only twice as large as the great hall in Lenardo's villa.

But where Lenardo's hall was light and decorated with bright colors, this room was paneled in dark wood that glinted softly in the torchlight. There was a fireplace, with a blaze that was somehow warm without being cheery, but there were no furnishings beyond a strip of rich, thick carpet on the floor leading up some steps to a platform, also thickly carpeted. On the platform was a throne—and on the throne lounged Maldek, leaning back with his right leg thrown across the padded arm of his throne. He thus leaned to the left, his left hand casually caressing an animal of some kind that sat in the shadows on the carpeted platform, leaning into his caresses just as Gray did for Torio.

When Gray saw the animal, he growled, and the beast opened surprising green eyes and chattered in a high-pitched voice.

Torio put a hand on Gray's head and silently ordered him to sit. Obediently, the dog did—but although his growls were no longer audible, Torio could feel them as vibrations in the dog's skull.

It took several commands for Maldek to silence the other animal's chattering—an ape of some sort, Torio recognized, as large as a man in the torso but with short dwarfed and bowed legs, so that its hands touched the ground when it stood. It was covered in thick reddish hair, except right around those strange eyes, and the disturbingly human hands.

Maldek was just as they had seen him in Dirdra's memory: very large and powerfully built, and dressed all in black. Tonight his robe was furred, with little of the silver embroidery they had seen before, but his face wore the same self-satisfied smile, chiseled perfection, carved in ice.

"Welcome to my castle," he greeted them in tones that attempted sincerity without warmth. "I trust my servants have treated you well. You deserve it—you passed all my tests with alacrity. I rarely find such worthy opponents."

"We have not come to oppose you, Maldek," Torio said. "Until you attacked us, we had no quarrel with you at all. Since we were able to defeat you at every turn, we will now consider—"

"Defeat?" The sorcerer laughed heartily. "You think you have defeated me, simply because you managed to get here through the obstacles? My dear Torio, the contest has not yet begun. Tell him, Zanos—you have merely passed the qualifying rounds to enter the games!"

"We are not here to play games," Torio began, but just then the doors to the chamber were opened once more, to admit the women.

Maldek rose to his feet. "Ah—the ladies. Please enter. The lovely Astra, wife of Zanos—you are a fortunate man, sir." He grinned lasciviously at the gladiator, and Torio Read Zanos quell his fighting instinct.

Astra was dressed in robes of a deep wine-colored velvet, trimmed in gray fur and encrusted with

garnets. Her hair was elaborately styled and en-
twined with velvet ribbons sparkling with the same
jewels.

Melissa was in gold velvet with dark brown fur
trim that matched her hair—which had been styled
so that part of it was braided and curled with
bands of gold mesh, but the rest hung loosely
down her back, displaying its natural curl. Her
dress was heavily encrusted with gold. "Melissa,"
said Maldek, "Reader and healer—but also a woman
of Adept powers. You have come to me to learn
how to expand those powers."

"Only in the direction of healing," she replied
warily, trying as Torio was to Read what the peculiar look in Maldek's eyes meant. But he was braced
against their Reading him.

After what seemed to Torio far too long a study
of Melissa, Maldek reached between her and Astra
to pull forward the woman half-hidden behind
them. "Dirdra!"

The Maduran woman's exquisite beauty was en-
hanced by a green velvet gown the exact color of
her eyes. Instead of fur, feathers in iridescent
greens decorated her robe. She was magnificently
beautiful, but deathly pale.

Maldek pulled her forward into the torchlight.
"Why, Dirdra, you haven't deserted us after all.
Look, Kwinn—your sister has come back to us!"

And as he spoke, the creature that had remained
crouched beside the throne, afraid to pass Gray to
follow its master, gave a great cry and fairly flew
across the room to hug Dirdra about the knees,
gasping painful sounds that they all knew now
were meant to be words of joyful greeting.

Dirdra dropped to her knees and wrapped her

arms about his shoulders, holding him close, her tears dropping like diamonds onto the trembling furred pelt as she whispered, "I couldn't leave you like this! Oh, Kwinn—I had to come back for you. I couldn't leave you in his evil power, my brother!"

Chapter Five

*W*hat the Readers wanted to do was examine Kwinn, but Maldek had other plans. First they were taken from the throne room to a banquet hall, where only the three who had used Adept powers did justice to the meal.

Maldek did not eat—causing Torio to Read the food carefully for drugs or poison. He could find nothing.

The Master Sorcerer came up behind him. "The game has not begun, Torio. You may safely enjoy the food provided. You are my guests now, and the rules of hospitality obtain."

For how long? Torio wondered, but Maldek did not respond. Gray voiced his opinion of their host's sincerity with a soft growl. It rose in volume when Maldek laid his hand on Torio's shoulder, but the dog didn't move. Without the healing fire, the last traces of Torio's injury vanished!

Melissa looked up, startled. "How did you do that?"

"Come and I will show you," the sorcerer replied. "Here"—he pointed to Torio's thigh without touching—"your friend has a deep puncture wound that has healed over, but will come to restrict those muscles if it is not soon healed cleanly."

"I planned to set it healing again tonight," Melissa replied. "By morning—"

"But there is no reason to wait so long," Maldek told her. "Put your hand over the wound."

Melissa did so—and Maldek placed his left hand over hers. Torio tried to Read what they did, but both the healer and the sorcerer braced to use Adept power. The healing fire touched his wound for a moment, but Maldek, his face between Melissa's and Torio's, murmured, "No—that way is long, and takes too much power. Like this."

This deeper wound took longer to heal—long enough for Torio to feel a strange cold sensation quite unlike the healing fire, as from the inside out the wound knitted together, clotted blood dissolving and dissipating.

He could Read what happened to his injury, but not how it was done. Melissa turned her face up to Maldek's. "Where . . . where did that power come from?" she asked. "I feel no weakness."

"Of course not," he replied, remaining just a moment too long with his hand over hers. Then he straightened. "There is a ready source of power—if one can tap it. You do, Melissa, but inefficiently. Try it on your other friend, Zanos. His wound still pains him."

Indeed, Torio had admired the gladiator's stoicism on the long day's ride, for he had to breathe shallowly to avoid pain, but deeply to keep moving with them. Yet he had not uttered a word of complaint.

Melissa put her hand over Zanos' wound . . . but nothing happened. She frowned, and healing warmth spread beneath her hand.

"No," said Maldek, beside her in one rapid stride. "Melissa, think of healing the wounded after a battle. Of how much use is a healer who falls asleep after treating twenty, when a hundred more are waiting?"

"It's not that I disagree, Lord Maldek," she replied. "It's that I cannot Read what you do to heal so quickly and cleanly."

"My master taught me by directing the power through my hands until I could control it. Here— try again."

Again he placed his hand over hers. When they lifted their hands, Zanos took a deep breath— without a stab of pain. "Thank you, Melissa," he said, but looked up at Maldek and continued, "I'll not thank *you*, Master Sorcerer. You owed me that—it was you who caused my wound!"

Maldek laughed. "Then we begin our contest even, point to point."

"Even? When you have powers beyond anything we've seen before?"

Maldek smiled his cold smile. "It disturbs you to find the tables turned, Zanos the Gladiator, undefeated Champion of the Aventine Games? How many men did *you* defeat with powers they could not understand?"

"Zanos!" Astra whispered sharply, putting her hand on her husband's arm. "Whatever he may be, we are his guests."

"Prisoners, you mean," the gladiator replied. "We could all end up like that poor creature!"

He gestured to where Dirdra sat, food untouched, cradling Kwinn's head in her lap.

"Ah, but Kwinn is happy," said Maldek. "He has what he wants now: his sister home again. Under my care, you will discover, everyone receives exactly what he wants."

"That's a lie!" Dirdra snapped. "Do you think Kwinn wanted to be turned into a mindless animal?"

"He wanted you to be well cared for, Dirdra . . . and he wanted to be with you. Now he has just that. And you, my dear, will soon give me what *I* want."

It was obvious that all were finished eating. Maldek bid them good night, and servants showed them to their rooms, all clustered in one wing of the castle.

As soon as the servants left them they all gathered in Dirdra's room, to examine Kwinn. Gray lay down in front of the door.

Astra was the only one of the group to have completed medical training at Gaeta, and she was also the most skilled among them at the fine discernment required to Read down to the level of nerve synapses and minute chemical changes.

"Dirdra, your brother's mind Reads something like that of a stroke victim," Astra said. "What Maldek has done is very cruel, but very easy given his combination of Reading and Adept talents. He has injured the part of Kwinn's brain that controls language—he can no longer find words for what he wants to think or say."

"Can he be cured?" Dirdra asked.

"I don't know," replied Astra. "I don't think I

could sort out and reconnect all those tiny fibers. Melissa?"

"It would be like trying to—" She searched for a less painful image than the one that came to mind, but Dirdra knew it already.

"To unscramble an egg," she said bitterly. She rocked her brother in her arms. "It was his mind Maldek took first. Only when that did not persuade me to come to him freely did he begin to amuse himself by twisting Kwinn's body."

Melissa shivered. "He has such power for healing! Why would he distort it to do deliberate harm?"

"As a demonstration of strength," said Zanos. "There doesn't seem to be anyone capable of opposing him—those empty beaches we passed to the south are an open invitation to an invading army."

"Oh, they've tried," said Dirdra. "Three years ago, Rokannia of the Western Isle sent a fleet of ships against Madura. Maldek did not even bother to raise the wind. He let the army come ashore, and met them with his minions—no army, just Maldek and some forty minor sorcerers against an army of over a thousand.

"Rokannia and her sorcerers sent fire and thunderbolts, but Maldek ignored them. Using his minions to shield him, he took her army, turned them orbu—and when Rokannia had exhausted herself he sent her own army against her. She was brought to his castle in chains, and there was a great celebration.

"Rokannia still rules the Western Isle, but she pays tribute in gold and grain every year. And it is rumored that every year when she comes to pay her tribute she begs Maldek to let her bear him a child to carry on his powers—but he refuses."

"I can see why you intrigue him so, Dirdra," said Zanos. "A Master Sorceress begs for his favors, but you spurn him."

"And what would you have me do?" she demanded. "Let him use me and cast me aside as he does his orbu?"

"Not at all," replied Zanos. "I spoke out of admiration for your courage."

"Besides," added Astra, "it is clear that Maldek does not want you unwilling—and he is too good a Reader not to know your feelings. What is intriguing is that he has never simply implanted the desire for him in your mind."

"It may be," Melissa said pensively, "that Maldek is just discovering that his power has limits."

"What do you mean?" asked Torio.

"He can have anything he wants," she replied, "except friendship . . . and love."

"He'll never have that in *this* land," said Dirdra. "The only people who want to be friends with Maldek are those who seek to profit by the association!"

Finally, since there was nothing they could do for Kwinn and Dirdra tonight, they retired to the rooms assigned them, and slept the sleep of utter exhaustion.

Torio woke in a cold sweat, out of a nightmare he could not remember. The castle was coming to life for the day. The guards were securing the drawbridge, which had just been let down, and servants scurried about, preparing for the awakening of their master and his guests.

When Torio sat up, Gray raised his head from where he had been sleeping at Torio's feet in the huge bed. "You were on the floor when I fell asleep," Torio informed him. "How did you get up here without waking me? Do you have Adept power, too?"

The dog stretched, then pushed his face under Torio's chin until the Reader rubbed the big shaggy head. That ritual completed, he jumped off the bed, went to the door, and whined. Torio opened the door for him, Reading the dog run down the stairs and across the courtyard, then over the drawbridge into the forest.

Apparently Gray's not worried about me this morning, thought Torio, and Read the other nearby rooms.

Dirdra was in the dull sleep of emotional exhaustion, her face still showing signs that after the others had left last night she had cried herself to sleep. Kwinn was curled up atop the coverings at her feet—just as Gray had been on Torio's bed.

Melissa still slept in her room across the hall, and next door Zanos and Astra were in one another's arms, her head on his shoulder, one arm about his waist as if her small body could shield his great one. On either side of the bed, their swords were hung within easy reach. *And what good are they against power like Maldek's?* Torio wondered.

He was Reading surfaces only, invading no one's privacy—but he was wide awake and too tense to go back to sleep. What was the "game" Maldek intended to play with them? And where was the Master Sorcerer now?

In another wing of the castle, he Read Maldek . . . also asleep. So, the man was human after all.

Torio had slept in the nightshirt he had found laid out on his bed. The clothes he had worn last night were gone, but an embroidered robe hung over the chair by the bed, fur-lined slippers beneath it.

More demonstrations of power: someone had been in and out of the room, not only without waking Torio, but without disturbing Gray.

Furthermore, just as Torio put on the robe and slippers, a servant started up the stairs from the kitchen with breakfast on a tray. The woman was Reading him—inexpertly enough that she instantly attracted his attention, but Reading nonetheless—yet when she reached his door she became blank to Reading for a moment, and the door opened by itself.

Someone with both Reading and Adept powers employed as a serving maid? Another symbol of Maldek's power.

"You be up early, young sir," the woman said as she laid the tray on the table. "Have a good breakfast, and then Devon will be up to help you dress. The Master says you be welcome to explore the castle till he rises. You may find summat of interest in his library."

"Thank you," Torio replied. The smell of fresh-baked bread was too good to resist. There was fruit mixed with soft farmer's cheese, as well, and a pot of fresh hot tea whose scent he did not recognize. As before, everything Read perfectly wholesome, so he ate and drank—and by that time Gray was back.

When the door opened by itself to admit the dog, Torio Read outward, amazed that anyone,

except perhaps Maldek, could have been Reading
the room without his knowing it.

But the man sweeping the dust out of the corners of the hall had been Reading the dog, not
Torio.

Gray eagerly accepted the leftovers of Torio's
breakfast. "But that's not enough for you," he
realized. "We'll go down to the kitchen and—" He
stopped, smiling grimly. "No—we don't even have
to ask!"

This time the door opened to admit a manser-
vant in Maldek's black-and-silver livery, followed
by a small boy with a platter of meat scraps and
bones, and a bowl of water. Hesitantly, he set
them before the huge dog, then scurried out of
the room.

Gray set happily to his meal while Devon laid
out clothing for Torio. The daytime garments were
no less rich than last night's robes, although the
hose were woolen, as was the undershirt. He was
given a satin shirt of an iridescent blue-green,
covered by a knee-length tunic of the same reddish-
brown wool as the hose, sleeveless and open-necked
to show the shirt. The tunic was belted in soft
leather.

Over that went a short fur vest, and then a
fur-trimmed ankle-length robe of the reddish-
brown wool, lined with blue-green satin.

Soft leather boots came up high on Torio's
calves—and fit as perfectly as if the cobbler had
measured his feet! Finally, Devon adjusted a soft
brimless hat on his head, something Torio was
quite unaccustomed to. Winter cloaks had hoods
where he came from, but no one required a head
covering indoors. Here, though, the castle's stone

walls gave off a chill not completely cut by the heavy hangings.

"Now, sir," said Devon, "you will be comfortable. Please feel free to explore. Perhaps the Master's library—?"

Why does Maldek want me in his library? Torio wondered. Perhaps it was a trap. For a Reader? Unlikely, as the lord of the castle must certainly know that his guests mistrusted him, and would be on guard.

So he dismissed Devon, deciding to remain right where he was—and Read the library.

It was a large room, with more books and scrolls than he had ever seen in one place. There was a desk with a huge candelabra, pens, a box of parchment, wax seals—Maldek or some secretary must work here regularly. The pens were trimmed and ready for use. The inkpot was freshly filled. The broad surface of the desk was clean of dust, and the wax droppings of the partly burned candles had been scraped away.

But the books and scrolls were what interested Torio. In Zendi, Master Clement was working with Aradia—who had lost her own library when her castle was destroyed—to build up a collection of useful works. How they would envy this library!

Unable to see, Torio had not learned to read—as opposed to Reading—until he could visualize. Once he had mastered the technique, though, he had read voraciously.

The other boys would never have put the effort into visualizing what they could see perfectly well, but Torio had to make the same effort to Read a page whether he opened the book or not—and so usually he didn't. The only way Lenardo had kept him from spending all his free time lying on his bed, lost in some book on the shelves of the Academy library, was to entice him with something more interesting.

Lenardo, whom he idolized, was the instructor of novice swordsmen. Since Torio, at age eight, imitated Lenardo in every way possible, his teacher had been able to entice the boy to exercise by introducing him to swordplay. As his body strengthened from the daily activity, he was able to play with the other boys, to learn to swim, and soon to be as sturdy and healthy as the other young Readers.

There had never seemed to be enough hours in the day for lessons and games *and* the books he wanted to explore. Torio was reminded, as he stretched out on his bed in Maldek's castle, of the nights Lenardo had discovered him reading instead of sleeping, and made him do the Readers' mental exercises for sleep.

With much the same sense of stealing time, Torio Read Maldek's library. The Master Sorcerer's own notebooks were stacked on the desk and on the shelves beside it, but Torio resisted the temptation to examine those first.

He found a section of works on medicine—herbal lore, surgery, diagrams of the bodies and brains of both humans and animals. Nearby were works on agriculture and horticulture, weather prediction . . . and a text on Adept climate manipulation. History, architecture, geography, Reading techniques, philosophy, government—Maldek seemed to have books on every topic.

Having discovered the library's organization, Torio turned to Maldek's notebooks, wondering

why the Master Sorcerer had left them in plain
sight. That had to be where the trap lay, if there
was one.

Maldek could not know which of his guests would
wake first this morning—nor would he probably
have guessed that Torio would not enter the library, although no skilled Reader would have *had*
to. Even Master Readers read with their eyes most
of the time.

Torio carefully assessed the books on the desk.
He found no physical traps. Moving them would
not trigger a trapdoor or a falling weight. There
was no poison on the covers or sprinkled within
the pages. . . .

Or was there?

The last entry in the top notebook was dated
yesterday:

> My visitors approach. They will be worthy
> opponents, for they have all survived. Even the
> hound has been turned to their advantage—
> although I saw in the blind one's mind that he
> knows nothing of animals. Had he shown fear
> or hate, the beast would have torn him apart.
>
> What powers have these five, that all have
> eluded my traps? They are weak, their pow-
> ers nothing to mine. I must know their secret.
> I must have this power they share.

Now that was interesting, that Maldek should
think they shared some secret power!

In an earlier entry, Torio found that someone
had Read Dirdra aboard the ship with them and
relayed the message to Maldek, who offered a
reward for such information. "I knew she would

return," he wrote. "I may be forced to restore her brother—but if I do, he will not be the same person. Still, Dirdra need not know that limit to my powers."

So if Dirdra had not arrived in the company of Readers who could warn of his treachery, Maldek would have led her on until he obtained what he wanted. Torio found the idea repellent. What kind of person would want the physical favors of someone who did not desire him?

It was not merely that Maldek was a Reader, and would know that Dirdra came to him unwillingly. None of Torio's nonReader friends would coerce someone to act against her will. He shied away from the mind of someone who could think like that.

Yet . . . if he did not come to understand the man, how could he help his companions escape Maldek's clutches?

So he continued to read.

And did not know he had fallen into the trap in the library until Gray became bored with sleeping on the fur rug beside the bed and jumped up to nudge Torio.

Pulling his mind out of Maldek's notes, he found that it was already midmorning. His companions were all gone from their rooms.

Torio swung his legs off the bed, Reading for the others. They were in the room where they had first met Maldek last night. The Master Sorcerer was once more on his throne.

A woman was being brought in through the courtyard, guarded—a Reader! In fact, a strong Reader who would have been a Magister, perhaps even a Master, in the Academy system.

//Who—?// the woman's mind questioned as Torio's thoughts touched hers. //You are Aventine!//

//Magister Torio, late of the Adigia Academy,// he told her in terms she would understand—for the flood of images her mind produced told him that she had come here from his homeland.

//Cassandra,// she identified herself, //once of Portia's Academy in Tiberium.//

Although Torio did not verbalize it, the woman Read his surprise that such a strong Reader was not ranked.

//I was once a Master Reader,// she told him, bitter shame shrouding her thoughts. //I broke my vows—and my life has been misery ever since.//

As Cassandra and Torio exchanged thoughts, she was being led by the guards toward Maldek's throne room, while Torio hurried down the stairs, Gray at his heels. He could Read Cassandra's reaction to being brought before Maldek: resignation, and the expectation of some new trouble piled upon a lifetime of the same. But she had no idea why she was here.

//Don't antagonize Maldek,// Torio warned as he Read that she cared little what happened to her now.

//You think he doesn't know anything he chooses?// the woman replied. //He Reads already who I am, and how much life has punished me, first for breaking my vows, then for fleeing to this land of evil.//

And Torio could, indeed, Read that the Master Sorcerer was following their mental conversation with avid interest.

Torio Read Astra stiffen, and turn to look as well as Read, but she was carefully guarding her thoughts so that only a strange turmoil of emotion could be Read from her.

Cassandra gave a despairing mental laugh as she was taken into the throne room. //I made one mistake in my life—and it destroyed the man I loved. Why should I be surprised if Maldek decides to add to my punishment?//

The Master Sorcerer rose as Cassandra was escorted in and stretched out a hand to beckon her forward. "Welcome, Cassandra," he said with the same guileless charm he had turned on Melissa the night before. "Have no fear—I have a wonderful surprise for you. Behold!"

As Torio took his place beside Melissa, Maldek dismissed the guards and motioned Astra forward. "As I promised—here you will find what you sought."

Astra moved stiffly, her mind refusing to believe—until she stood face to face with Cassandra. Torio heard Zanos gasp as the two women stood in profile: the same lines, as alike as the two faces formed by the drawing of a wine goblet.

Cassandra stared blankly at Astra—but the younger woman whispered, "You . . . you are my mother!"

Cassandra blinked, then stepped back and glared at Maldek. "This is some trick for your evil satisfaction!"

"Indeed not," replied the sorcerer. "It is for *your* satisfaction, Cassandra—but especially for your daughter's."

"I have no daughter," the woman insisted. "My first child died soon after birth . . . and later I bore my husband two stillborn sons. The gods punished us for our transgressions."

"Cassandra," said Astra, "I *am* your daughter, Astra. Portia lied to you. When you were weak after childbirth, your Reading powers diminished, she used the techniques designed to heal sick minds . . . but to evil purpose. She made you think that you Read your own child dead."

"But . . . why?" Cassandra asked. "Portia had no reason to lie to me."

"She wanted to keep your child in her power. I am the daughter of two Master Readers. Portia led me to believe that you had deserted me, so that I would turn to her as a mother. But when I grew up, my Reading powers increased—and I discovered how she had lied to me. And to you . . . Mother."

Cassandra stared. "I Read that you are telling the truth . . . at least as you know it." Tears slid down her cheeks. "Oh, child, whether you are truly my daughter or no, I have brought the curse of the gods upon you if your search for me brought you to this place of evil!"

Astra blushed. "I . . . did not come seeking you," she admitted. "I had no way to trace where you might have gone. I came here with my husband, who—"

"Husband!" exclaimed Cassandra, looking past Astra to Zanos, Reading his clumsy effort to follow their thoughts as well as their words. "Yes . . . he is a Dark Moon Reader, but surely you inherited enough powers—?" Her eyes widened as she Read Astra's tumbled thoughts. "You . . . you ran away from Portia to marry this man? You broke your vows, too? Oh, child—why did you have to inherit my weakness?"

"You don't understand!" said Astra. "Mother—

please come with Zanos and me. Let us tell you our story." She turned to the Master Sorcerer, who was watching the reunion with keen interest. "Maldek, I think I have had in the back of my mind this whole journey that somewhere I might find news of my parents . . . even find them alive. And so I thank you."

The sorcerer smiled with apparent sincerity. "It is my pleasure, Astra. By all means, go have a private talk with your mother. Melissa, if you will come with me, I will continue to teach you what you seek. Dirdra—"

"I will walk in the forest with my brother," she replied.

"Then, Torio—?"

"I'll come with you, if you don't object," he told Maldek. "I may have no Adept powers, but perhaps I can help Melissa Read just what happens when you heal people."

They went into a long, hall-like room on the ground floor. It faced the courtyard, where it was safe to have large, many-paned windows to admit sunlight. In the morning, when all the fires but the cooking fire were out, it was the warmest room in the castle.

This was the infirmary. Although it was clean, Torio could tell that it was seldom used. There were only two beds set up with fresh straw mattresses, although he could Read frames for a dozen or more stacked in a nearby storage room.

In Wulfston's castle, and in Lilith's, at least a dozen beds were always available, frequently occupied with people in healing sleep. There were healers in every village, but people whose illness or injury was beyond the powers of such minor

Adepts were always taken to the Lord Adept. Here, it appeared, the Lord of the Land rarely bothered with his people's needs.

Or perhaps it was the payment he exacted that made people fear to come. The guards had to drag in a man all bent and crippled with rheumatism. Despite pain that made the Readers wince, he flung himself at Maldek's feet, saying, "Master, I dinna ask to be brought here. Please, Master—I be content!"

"But wouldn't you be happier without your pain?" asked Maldek. With a wave of his hand, the man's pain disappeared.

"Now," said Maldek as the man stared down at his body as if he'd never seen it before, "we must cool the inflammation and straighten those limbs."

The guards lifted the patient onto one of the beds, where he clutched at the mattress with his poor bent hands and asked, "What do ye want of me, Master?"

"Why, nothing but to make you well," Maldek told him. "You will be cured—and then you will be able to work. Instead of begging in the streets, you will pay your tithe to my support, which is the support of my people. Rest now," he added, touching the man on the forehead, at which he promptly fell asleep.

Maldek's rationale was precisely what Torio had heard Aradia say as to why it was in the best interest of a Lord Adept to expend his energies in healing. But the unused state of the infirmary and the reaction of his patient showed that this was not Maldek's usual practice.

"Now, Melissa," said the Master Sorcerer, "show me how you would heal this man."

"I have done this kind of healing before," she replied. "The poor man's body is fighting itself." She lifted one of the gnarled hands, Read it, and then became blank to Reading as she concentrated. Healing heat spread beneath her fingers. The inflammation yielded, dissolved away, and the swelling went down as improved circulation carried away the accumulated fluid.

"I can make the muscles relax," she said, "but after he becomes accustomed to being without pain it will take exercise to bring his limbs back to full function. The tendons have shortened; only time and use will lengthen them."

Maldek Read Melissa's work, Torio Reading with him. So far he had seen no sign that their host was a better Reader than he was, nor did the examination of the patient's hand give any such indication.

"You have done your work well, Melissa," said Maldek, "but you have wasted too much of your own energy. Tell me—do you know what Adept powers are?"

Melissa studied him, looking puzzled. "I don't think you mean that they are powers to affect material objects with the mind."

"No—I mean what they *are*, not what they do."

"Then I don't know," Melissa replied.

"They are forces from a different realm," replied Maldek. "We can use them to catalyze our own efforts, which is what most Adepts do—or we can simply guide them, let them pour through us, and thus use very little of our own energy. That is what Master Sorcerers do."

"A different realm?" questioned Torio. "What do you mean? Another plane of existence? Such planes are not physical, and can only be reached out of body. How can they provide power?"

Maldek smiled disarmingly at him. "An excellent question. You have ventured onto other planes of existence, Torio? You are very young for such a quest—it is said that one is hardly rooted in this world until he has lived in it for a generation— thirty years."

"And I suppose *you* waited that long?" asked Torio.

"Almost," replied Maldek, frowning. "Do they teach you this in your Academy training while you are so young? That is dangerous—you could lose yourself."

"It is not something I would do for amusement," Torio replied. "One of my teachers was lost on the planes of existence, and it took a circle of Readers and Adepts to draw him back. I know of others who have been lost forever, their bodies left behind to die.

"But you are avoiding my question, Maldek. One does not enter the planes of existence in his body, for they are immaterial. So how can they have anything to do with physical power?"

"How? That is something I do not know. *That* there are planes of power, though, I am witness to. And those planes must be tapped while one is *in* the body. Out of it, one cannot control them—or at least no one ever has except in legend."

"The ghost-king," Torio identified.

"It is legend here in Madura, too," replied Maldek. "Even if that tale is not pure fable, in living memory no one has tapped the planes of power out of body. Our version of the legend says that when the king did so, the power flowed through his conscious link with his helpless body, and destroyed it. That is how he *became* a ghost."

"That part's not in our story," said Torio. "But . . . how can you reach other planes of existence without going out of body? And how can you Read and use Adept powers at the same time?"

"I'm not Reading when I do it," Maldek replied. "That is why I can teach Melissa only as I was taught—and until you develop the Adept half of your powers, I cannot teach it to you, Torio. But this is what Melissa came here to learn. Let her learn it."

"Go ahead," Torio replied. "I'll try to Read what you're doing."

But it was the same as the night before—he could Read what happened to the man's arthritic joints, but not the source of the change.

Perhaps he found it difficult to concentrate on the healing because he was too aware of Maldek touching Melissa. In fact, he was Reading the Master Sorcerer so closely that when he stood behind her, wrapping his huge body around hers to put his hands over hers on the patient, Torio could smell Melissa's fresh scent in Maldek's nostrils.

And Maldek's reaction—the reaction of a normal, healthy man to having his arms around a beautiful woman.

Torio gritted his teeth and concentrated on the healing. As before, it seemed to take place spontaneously, without the healing fire. Not only did the inflammation disappear, but the muscles relaxed and the shortened tendons . . . *grew*!

Torio could not believe what he was Reading.

Healers had used traction in the Aventine Empire, when normal exercise would not restore full function. Adepts might work on deformed limbs daily, making small progress each time until they were restored—but he had never Read anything like this. Of course Melissa had to learn it!

But, "I just don't know what you're *doing*!" she protested when Maldek took his hands off hers for the dozenth time, and for the dozenth time the healing stopped abruptly.

"It's all right," he said. "I couldn't do it when I first tried, either. It will come with practice, Melissa. But now, Read your patient."

Both Torio and Melissa did so. The man was sleeping quietly, all inflammation gone from his joints, muscles relaxed, connective tissue restored to normal. He would require food and exercise to restore his strength—but then he would be able to resume a normal life!

"Now Read me," Maldek instructed.

"I'm tired just from concentrating," exclaimed Melissa, "and you're as fresh as if you'd just had a good night's sleep!"

"I did not use my own energy," Maldek explained. "In fact, I sometimes think that the more one draws from the planes of power, the more one is energized by what one touches. Come—we have another patient waiting."

This time the patient walked in willingly, looking around, taking stock. He was a red-haired man in his early thirties, dressed in fine fabrics, but of too many different bright colors. Arrogantly, he looked Maldek up and down, then asked, "Well, Master Sorcerer, what did you really have your guardsmen bring me here for? I'll never believe it was this!"

And he thrust out his right arm—which ended not in a hand, but a hook!

Torio gasped in recognition. "By the gods!"

"Oh, no, Torio," said Maldek, "the gods had nothing to do with it. I *knew* where this one was. It was Cassandra who was hard to find."

"What's going on here?" the red-haired man asked. "Them guards told me you wanted me at the castle to get a new hand. I told 'em you don't do favors for gamblers—so what's it really about?"

"Exactly what the guards told you," Maldek replied. "I sent them for you in particular, and also told them to bring in the most crippled beggar they saw in the streets." He waved toward the sleeping man. "As you can see, he is no longer crippled. I have a student here learning to heal. I plan to demonstrate on you."

"Yeah?" the man questioned. "I'm not so sure I like that. You gonna grow my hand back? Welchers are scared pretty bad by this hook."

"And also people you 'protect' for a fee, no doubt," said Maldek. "But I will have another surprise for you soon, Bryen. And I want you in perfect condition for it."

"No thanks!" said Bryen, and headed for the door. "I've always stayed out of your way, Maldek. You got no call to pick me for your experiments."

"Ah, but I have," replied the sorcerer—and Bryen stopped in his tracks, paralyzed. "Come now—I've no reason to hurt you. I'm doing you a favor."

But not Zanos, Torio thought to himself. If there was any form of human parasite Zanos hated, it was gamblers. Could Maldek know that?

Released, Bryen turned, anger and fear clashing within him. "What you gonna want in return for the favor I never asked for?" he demanded. "I got no woman I care about—don't pay in *this* land! You need more money? I can get it for you, depending—"

"Bryen, I am *not* asking you to pay. You are doing a favor for two of my guests. Now lie down, and let me restore your hand."

Bryen stared at Melissa and Torio as he moved reluctantly to the empty bed. "Your guests, huh? You folks from some other country?"

"As a matter of fact, we are," said Melissa.

"Well—take care who you think's your friend," Bryen warned.

"Just go to sleep now and let us work," said Maldek, and the red head dropped onto the pillow.

Maldek removed the tight wrappings which secured the hook to the stump of Bryen's right arm. The arm itself was as strong as his left—he obviously used the hook, probably just as he had suggested.

The pale stump was cleanly healed over, long calloused and without pain.

"Observe," said Maldek, "what you will be able to do once you have mastered the planes of power."

Torio and Melissa Read together. Maldek became blank to Reading as he asserted his Adept powers, then Readable again as he studied the effects, removing the calluses and scar tissue, leaving only normal flesh at the end of Bryen's arm— soft and pink and vulnerable.

But then Maldek began to Read with fine discernment, down to the very level of the cells of Bryen's body. Torio had Read thus with Astra, knew Lenardo could have Read it . . . but he had never tried to Read to such a level on his own.

At least in this skill, Maldek *was* a better Reader
. . . now. But Torio's powers would grow for ten
years yet. Meanwhile, Reading with Maldek would
give him experience against the day when his own
powers would reveal such depths.

But then . . . Maldek began to Read *inside* the
cells!

Down, down, into the tangled strands of life
itself, Maldek reached and manipulated. Lost, Torio
observed without understanding. Maldek spread
cold white fire among the dancing threads until
they writhed and intermeshed in new patterns—
blinking in and out as Maldek stopped Reading to
control, then resumed to study his results.

Then he withdrew, and stood Reading the stump
of Bryen's arm, just within the flesh. Here Torio
could Read for himself . . . and observed a miracle.

The sealed-off bone ends dissolved, and cell by
cell the bones began to extend. At the same time,
tiny bits of new living matter formed out of the
old, and assembled themselves at the ends of the
two bones of the forearm.

Melissa gasped as she recognized the pattern.
//It's like the hand of a baby growing in the
womb—so tiny, yet all the elements in place!//

Indeed, the formation was so small that it was
not visible even as a swelling . . . but it was *there*!

Maldek guided the substance until it had taken
on a life of its own. Then he let go his concentration and stood back, breathing heavily.

"You're tired," said Melissa.

"Only weary with concentration," the Master Sorcerer replied. "Let Bryen sleep. We'll waken him
to feed him later—for his body will deplete itself
with all the work it must do."

"The substance, then," Torio asked, "comes from Bryen's body?"

"Of course. It is possible to make matter disintegrate, Torio, but I've never yet heard of the Master Sorcerer who could create it. And the pattern of Bryen's whole body, including his missing hand, is in every cell. All I had to do was copy it."

They went to dinner, then—just the three of them, for Dirdra had not returned, and Zanos and Astra, still closeted with Cassandra, requested that the meal be sent up to their room.

"When are you going to tell Zanos that his brother is here?" asked Torio.

"As soon as Bryen has enough strength for the reunion—just a few days. Zanos is not a strong Reader—surely you two can keep from spoiling my surprise?"

"Of course," Melissa replied, assuming Torio's consent. "Besides, it's Astra's day today, finding her mother after all these years. Let them enjoy their reunion, and when Bryen has recovered Astra will be able to share Zanos' happiness the way he is sharing hers today."

Torio wondered if they were indeed happy, considering how bitter Cassandra had seemed—but when she came down to supper with Zanos and Astra that evening she was a changed woman. Her eyes and Astra's both showed that they had cried—but they were happy now.

Face on, Cassandra and Astra did not look nearly as much alike as they did in profile, although it was easy to guess they were related. But when they smiled—

Although Torio felt that no woman could compare in beauty to Melissa, with her delicate heart-

shaped face and softly curling hair, he knew that
other women were beautiful as well. Lilith had a
serene, classic beauty. Aradia was exotically lovely.
But Astra was not a beautiful woman, merely pretty
in the way of youth, and Cassandra had not even
that.

But when they smiled, both mother's and daughter's faces took on such a glow that for that moment they seemed the most beautiful women in
the world.

Over supper, Cassandra told an abbreviated version of the life's story she had revealed to her
daughter and son-in-law that day.

She had, indeed, broken her vows as a Master
Reader, as had Master Anthony. When Cassandra's
pregnancy revealed their indiscretion, the Council
of Masters decreed that oath-breakers were not to
be rewarded with one another, but that they would
be separated and sent to the far ends of the empire.

So Cassandra and Anthony decided to run away
together.

But Portia watched Cassandra too closely. The
day she packed her belongings, she found the
door blocked by the Master of Masters—and there-
after locked. With her advancing pregnancy, it
became less and less possible for her to flee.

Anthony, pursued as he moved from village to
village trying to find a way to rescue Cassandra,
was eventually forced to cross the border into the
savage lands.

Finally Cassandra's baby was born—and died.
At least so Portia had made her believe. And in
her despair, Cassandra fled—perhaps escaping too
easily, she thought now that she knew Portia had
not wanted her, but her child.

In the savage lands Cassandra had to hide her Reading ability, for the savages, terrified of their powers, killed Readers. For almost a year she had wandered, terrified, until at last she touched minds with another at a harvest fair—and found her love.

They spoke their marriage vows to one another, and decided to travel northward, to where they had heard of verdant isles where people of both Reading and Adept powers lived in peace.

"And indeed," Cassandra finished, "Madura was such a land in those days. We sailed here eagerly, and found welcome. It seemed that we had paid for our misdeeds, and that at last we could settle down to good lives.

"But . . . our children were born dead, and we knew the punishment of the gods was still upon us. We lived far in the northern hills of this island, seeking obscurity among the shepherds—and then the old Lord of the Land died."

She looked at Maldek, and continued, choosing her words carefully. "At first, things seemed the same as always, except that the shepherds complained that the new Master Sorcerer demanded twice as many sheep and three times as much wool as his portion of their goods. But they had fine flocks, and it was little hardship for them.

"Then . . . the tithe was increased, and demands came for young men of the village for the army, and young women. . . ." She let that trail off. "Then a few years ago the climate changed. Winters became longer. The newborn lambs died in the snow, and the sheep that survived grew weaker as there was less and less for them to eat.

"Anthony went out with the shepherds in a blizzard, to find and rescue as many of their sheep as possible. None of us were strong anymore—we were suffering shortages as much as the sheep were. Anthony stayed out all night with the shepherds—and caught pneumonia. So did several other men. The village healer exhausted himself, while I did all that I could with herbs—but it had been years since I could get many herbs I needed. Five good men died that winter . . . among them Anthony."

Cassandra fell silent. Maldek rose and came up behind her chair, placing his hand on her shoulder. "Cassandra—I am only beginning to recognize what harm I have done in my attempts to strengthen Madura against its enemies. If I could bring your husband back, I would—but you know I cannot."

"No," Dirdra suddenly spoke up, "you can only make orbu, you fiend!"

"And I have stopped doing that," Maldek replied, irritation edging his voice for a moment. Then he calmed himself. "You have no reason to believe me, Dirdra—how could you, when it is your own example that has shown me my mistakes only in these past few days?"

Torio tried to Read the man's sincerity, but he was shielding his emotions by bracing for Adept power—Melissa did that sometimes when she didn't want Torio to know how she felt, but in Maldek he suspected it was something more.

Maldek, meanwhile, said to Cassandra, "Although I cannot restore your husband, at least I have reunited you with your daughter. It is not recompense; there can be no recompense. But I shall

restore the land, and reunite those whom I can—
and perhaps, one day, my people will forgive me."

"You *are* your people," Torio suddenly found
himself saying. "And you are your land, Maldek.
The land may demand your life to restore it."

The Master Sorcerer stared at him. "That is so,"
he replied. "But how do you know this, Torio?"

"He has the gift of prophecy," Melissa replied.
"But Torio, you said the land *may* demand Maldek's
life."

"There is yet time," the words tumbled forth,
"but it is growing short. Make your words true,
Maldek, or only one who dies your death for you
can save you and your land."

Chapter Six

"**B**ut what does it *mean*?" Melissa demanded of Torio after the group at supper had broken up. "First you said that Maldek might have to die for his land—and then you said someone else might have to die his death. I don't understand."

"And you think I do?" Torio asked. "How could someone die somebody else's death? All I know is that Maldek gives me cold chills—because he hasn't really reformed."

"Is that a prophecy, too?"

They had walked out into the forest with Gray. Torio picked up a stick and tossed it. The dog loped after it and brought it back while Torio sorted his thoughts.

"No, it's not a prophecy; it's a feeling. *You* try to Read him when he's making an apology—he's hiding his true feelings.

"I could tell that he's heard before that the Lord is the land, and may have to restore it with his own blood—only I'll wager he never thought it would apply to *him* until he realized what he'd done to the beautiful, rich land that Zanos and Cassandra remember. Now he's frightened, and he's trying to make amends. But Maldek doesn't strike me as really wanting to change. He enjoys controlling people."

"Don't be so cynical, Torio. People *do* reform."

"Not the ones who have tasted power. Portia went down fighting, remember? Besides—Maldek's reform is too quick. He couldn't have changed overnight."

"I don't think it was overnight," said Melissa, fending off Gray as he almost knocked her over begging her to play with him. She tossed the stick for him. "I think Maldek has been dissatisfied for a long time with the way his power has separated him from other people, but he didn't know what was wrong until he watched the five of us together. We're like a family, you know—Dirdra is here because of her brother, and Zanos is looking for his. So now Maldek is trying to bring families together—and he likes the feeling of using his powers for good. Torio, you can't tell me you haven't Read how Maldek feels when he's healing!"

"He feels pride in his power," Torio agreed. "He's showing off for you, Melissa."

She stopped abruptly. "Torio—you can't be *jealous*, can you?"

"Do I have reason to be?" he countered.

"No!" she replied. A little too quickly? Then, "I'm tired," she said. "It will be dark soon. Let's go back."

Torio refrained from reminding her that they were both Readers, to whom darkness meant nothing, and simply turned to walk with her back toward the castle.

Apparently they had been waited for. The moment they crossed the drawbridge, it was hauled up with a horrible rumbling sound. Torio shuddered, and Gray nudged his hand as if to give comfort.

"What's wrong?" asked Melissa.

"Nothing," he replied. "I think—yes, the sound reminds me of that stone sliding down out of the quarry onto that young man Wulfston and I rescued. It makes me think of someone being crushed to death."

"Auf! Don't say such things!" she said.

"It's not a prophecy—it's something that happened in the past." Then he turned to face her. "But—my gift of prophecy disturbs you, doesn't it? Every time I say something about the future, you withdraw from me. Melissa, I can't *help* it."

"I know," she replied. "Still . . . it's frightening, Torio. And this time you prophesied death!"

"Only if Maldek doesn't mend his ways."

"But you don't think he can. You think he'll have to die—or that one of us will have to die for him!"

The next day, Maldek and his guests rode into the city. Torio Read apphrehension flowing ahead of the party as word spread that the Master Sorcerer was in town.

Mothers called their daughters into back rooms.

Beggars scurried into corners and huddled, shaking, hoping not to be noticed—for one of their number had been carried off to the castle yesterday, and no one knew what had become of him.

They left their horses at a stable and proceeded on foot to the local hospital, where the healers looked up in astonishment, not believing they had Read the Lord of the Land approaching. They tried to shield their thoughts by bracing for Adept power, but Torio caught the fact that Maldek had turned away their pleas for his aid years before. Without the help of such a powerful Adept, the healers were severely limited—hence the presence of beggars like the crippled man Maldek and Melissa had cured yesterday.

In a private consultation room, a mother held her little girl on her lap while a female healer told her, "Try to take her to Rokannia of the Western Isle, when she comes here to pay tribute. She has the power to heal the nerves and allow your child to see."

It was the same degenerative condition that had caused Torio to be born blind—a fairly common ailment which any of the Lords Adept in the Savage Empire could cure with a few weeks of daily treatments, as long as it was corrected in infancy. As the child grew older, such treatments were less and less effective, and for adults they didn't work at all.

The healer looked up in astonishment as Maldek walked into the private room without knocking.

"Master!" gasped the mother, falling to her knees and clutching her child to her breast as if she feared it would be torn from her grip. The baby, naturally, began to scream.

"Give me the child," said Maldek.

"Master, please!" said the healer. "This is Moradee's only child. You surely have no use for a blind infant. Please don't take her away!"

"Take her away?" Maldek asked. "Is that what they say of me in my land—that I steal babes from their mothers? No, woman—give me the child that I may heal her."

Trembling, the mother delivered the screaming baby into Maldek's huge hands. He slung her easily onto one arm, her head in his hand, her body along his forearm, and stroked her brow. She fell asleep at once.

Torio Read Maldek Reading for the defective nerves—then that amazing cold white fire—and the fibers grew in moments, generating the necessary tissue and connections.

What would have taken Wulfston or Aradia weeks of daily treatments was completed by Maldek in less than a quarter of an hour. Then he placed the infant back in her mother's arms and touched her on the forehead.

The child's eyes opened, and she made a gurgling sound. Torio could Read that the little girl's sight was restored, but there was no way for the mother to know.

The baby had never seen before. She couldn't focus her eyes, or recognize her mother's face.

But the healer picked up a lighted candle, held it in front of the child's face, and then moved it to the side.

The child's head turned, following the light. She let out a happy chortle and reached toward it, but the healer held the candle safely out of reach.

The mother broke into sobs. "Oh, Master—thank you! How can I ever repay you?"

"There is no need," Maldek replied. "Healer—have you any other patients who require my skills?"

"Not at present, Master," she replied hesitantly.

"When you have, send them to my castle."

"Yes, Master," the healer replied—but Torio

knew Maldek Read as easily as he did that she
feared some underlying scheme beneath the Master Sorcerer's apparent kindness. And he felt
Maldek's annoyance at her distrust.

But Maldek held himself in check as he showed
them the rest of the hospital facility, which was
similar to the one in Zendi. Then he suggested,
"You may wish to explore my city on your own—
and as you all have the inner sight, I have no fear
you will become lost and unable to find your way
back to the stable where we left our horses."

Dirdra had not come with them on this excur-
sion, for Kwinn screamed and clung to her every
time she tried to leave his sight, and the city was
certainly no place for him—or for Gray, who had,
amazingly, seemed to understand Torio's instruc-
tion to stay behind, although he made clear that
he was not happy about it.

Zanos and Astra took Cassandra off to explore,
while Melissa wanted to go to the herb market.

Maldek seemed determined to stay with Melissa,
so Torio followed along, trying to decide if he was
Reading a growing rivalry with Maldek, or only
imagining it.

When Melissa was deep in discussion with one
of the herbalists over the uses of some medicines
she was unfamiliar with, Torio asked Maldek,
"Couldn't you cure Kwinn with the same technique you used on that baby?"

"No—but I could cure you, if you like."

"No, thank you," Torio answered automatically.

Maldek cocked his head to one side, studying
the young Reader. "Why not? It *is* convenient to
see, Torio—and perhaps if you did not have to
stumble in the dark at any time you are not Read-

ing, you would be able to release your Adept powers, as Melissa has done."

"I'm not sure I want such powers," Torio told him, and knew that Maldek Read his thought that the Master Sorcerer was only one example of the wrong that could be done with them.

But Maldek chose another direction for their conversation. "You are the only one whose desires I cannot fathom. What do you want of me, Torio?"

"Nothing."

"Then if you refuse to take from me, what do you seek in these isles?"

"Adventure, perhaps—although I've had enough of that for the moment, thank you."

"A typical young man's answer," Maldek observed, "but not yours, I think. Can it be that you are not seeking something to be found here, but to escape something at home?"

"A shrewd guess, Maldek," Torio replied. "I left my homeland to avoid becoming a Lord of the Land. Like you."

For the first time in two days, the cold, mocking smile played over Maldek's lips. "We are kin at heart, then—for you recognize as well as I that power must be exercised in order to rule. It is sometimes necessary to be harsh."

"Firm," Torio corrected. "A difficult line to tread. My teacher, Master Lenardo, treads it as easily as Lord of the Land as he did as teacher in the Academy—but I do not want responsibility for other people's lives. Even as a teacher, my mistakes hurt other people."

"And so you remain blind when you could see, weak when you could be strong? You are a fool, Torio. You place yourself at other people's mercy."

"We are all at the mercy of the gods," Torio replied, falling back on an Aventine commonplace.

"When I meet your gods, I will believe in them," Maldek retorted. "Meanwhile, I will rely on my own powers."

"Call it the gods, call it fate—there is something beyond the powers of mere men," Torio told him. "I have seen prophecies come true—and I see my own happening, even now. I told Zanos he would find his brother, and that his brother would have his hand again—and you have found Bryen and restored his hand. Perhaps, then, you believe that I am controlling you?"

Maldek laughed. "That is something no man will ever do! Don't try it, Torio. And be grateful . . . I seldom give my opponents a warning."

"Why have you made us opponents?" Torio asked. "We did nothing to you, made no challenge. And Dirdra and her brother—why do you aid Zanos' brother and not Dirdra's? Dirdra is your subject; Zanos is not."

"The game is not finished," Maldek answered.

"Does that mean you *will* cure Kwinn? Surely the method you are using to regrow Bryen's hand would work."

"Yes—it would restore his intelligence, but not his memories or his . . . self. He would be like a newborn baby, having to learn everything again. And since the circumstances would be quite different, he would probably become a considerably different person."

"Have you told Dirdra that?" asked Melissa, who had come up just in time to hear this last exchange. "She ought to know that you cannot restore her brother as she knew him. However, I think that she would gladly undertake the task of teaching him, if you would return his understanding."

The moment Melissa's attention was back on him, Maldek's charm returned. "You are right, Melissa. I will tell her."

"And restore Kwinn—as much as you are capable of?" she pursued.

He looked down at her, speculation in his blue eyes, thoughts carefully shielded. "Would you like me to do that?"

"I would like to see Dirdra obtain what she has made such a long, hard journey for. You said we would each receive what we had come for, Maldek. You are teaching me your healing skills. You have reunited Astra with her mother, and brought Zanos' brother to him. What did you plan for Dirdra, if not to restore Kwinn?"

"What does she plan for me?" he countered. "Do you think she owes me nothing?"

"Her loyalty," said Melissa, "as your subject— which she has already shown you by returning, even though you had abused her and her family."

"She returned for her brother, not for me."

"Then *gain* her respect and loyalty by restoring him!" exclaimed Melissa. "If you won't, once I have learned to reach that healing power you have shown me, I will use it to restore Kwinn myself. And if I cannot learn it, I heard what the healer at the hospital said about sending people she can't cure to Rokannia. I'm sure she would help Kwinn."

"You would defy me, Melissa?" Maldek asked.

"I am not your subject—I came to this land seeking knowledge. You have freely offered me that knowledge. If you now wish to rescind that offer—"

"No, I do not. When we return to the castle, you shall have another lesson. But now, let us go to the guild hall and see how plans are progressing for Rokannia's visit."

"Is she coming soon?" asked Torio.

"In twelve days. My people will celebrate our victory, in which none of them died. You must admit that there I have achieved something no other Lord of the Land ever has: although I maintain an army as a secondary defense, I no longer have to send them into battle. In my land, mothers need no longer fear that their sons will be called to die."

No, thought Torio, *only that they will be turned into mindless automatons*. But he ceased Reading as he thought it, so that Maldek would not catch his thought—and in that moment while he was blind, a cart rumbled by in the busy street.

The sound was magnified by the enclosing stone buildings, and for one moment, not Reading, Torio felt again the horror of being crushed to death—

"Torio!"

Melissa grasped his hand and pulled him out of the way. "You were going to walk right into that wagon! What thought is so important to keep hidden?"

Of course he resumed Reading immediately, and found Maldek's face saying, "I told you so," even though he did not broadcast the thought. There was something else in the Master Sorcerer's eyes, too—some speculation that made Torio wince in anticipation. But how could he be more vigilant than he already was?

            *   *   *

In the middle of the night, Torio woke with a start in a cold sweat, absolute terror clutching his gut.

Gray came and licked his face, and he clung to the dog, taking comfort in the warm, unquestioning reality of the creature.

The dream was gone. He could not remember anything but mindless terror. All he knew was that it was a dream he had had often as a child—a dream laden with guilt, as if all the horrors of the world were to be laid at his door.

But he could never remember it, and as he grew up it came less frequently, and only at times of stress. He had dreamed it after the battle at Adigia, in which Decius lost his leg, and again after the earthquake at Gaeta and the fall of Tiberium.

Each time he had dreamed it when something he had said or done had ended in harm. But yesterday—he could not remember anything he had said or done that had hurt anyone. Was he afraid of having antagonized Maldek? Perhaps that was it. Whether the Master Sorcerer's attempts to reform were sincere or for some ulterior purpose, what did it matter as long as people were healed and none were turned orbu—at least for a time? He should put aside his skepticism, and allow Maldek's people whatever benefits the Lord of their Land might give them, however temporary.

Three days later, Bryen's hand was the size of a half-grown child's, and he could move it freely. "It will simply grow now, until it reaches normal size in a few weeks," Maldek told him.

"So now what?" Bryen asked, looking from the hand up at Maldek. "I can't believe you done this just for my sake."

"As a matter of fact, I didn't do it for *you* at all," Maldek explained. "Come with me, Bryen. There is someone I want you to meet."

Zanos was with Torio in the courtyard, practicing with broadswords—and winning easily because Torio's attention was divided.

"What's the matter with you today?" the gladiator asked. "You're giving me no more challenge than Gray could, trying to wield a sword with his teeth!"

At the mention of his name, Gray woofed and wagged his tail. The first time he had seen Zanos apparently attack Torio he had come between them, growling and threatening—but Torio had finally made him understand that it was a game, so now he sat and watched, waiting for his turn to play.

Knowing that Maldek and Melissa were bringing Bryen to the courtyard, Torio let himself concentrate on the match and began to give Zanos a bit of competition. The broadsword was a much better weapon for the gladiator's strength than for Torio's speed, but Zanos insisted every man ought to know how to fight with whatever weapon was at hand, so Torio swung and ducked, and almost caught Zanos off guard with a feint, drawing a delighted laugh from the gladiator.

"That's the way! But a good broadswordsman would—" He came in under Torio's guard—but the younger man jumped back and pivoted, swinging sideways at Zanos' exposed biceps.

The gladiator whirled just in time and took the

blow on his heavy chest padding, bringing him
within reach of Torio's neck.

The practice sword merely stung, but Torio protested, "That move would work in the arena, or
any time you're wearing armor—but if you weren't
shielded, my strike would have killed you."

"If I weren't shielded, I wouldn't have allowed
you so close," Zanos replied. "But I concede—we
hadn't defined whether we were supposedly wearing armor or not."

"I've never worn armor," said Torio. "You have
two sets of reflexes, Zanos—one for arena-style
combat and one for other fighting. How do you
keep them apart?"

"Reflexes aren't enough. You know that," laughed Zanos, with a stabbing blow that Torio easily
parried. "You're thinking all the time, Torio—but
at the same time you act without deliberating. You
have a natural talent—I could have made a gladiator out of you!"

Zanos thrust. Torio deflected his sword and
swung again—but his arms were growing tired
after a long exercise with the weighted practice
broadsword. Zanos could probably go on all day.

He Read Zanos Read his fatigue and start to lay
on, driving Torio back toward the wall. The Reader
retreated, merely keeping up his guard and trying
to let his muscles revive for—

One last flurry of blows!

Zanos grinned as Torio turned on him. "Good!
Very good! *I* would have you, with my strength—
but unless you came up against another gladiator,
you'd win with that strategy, Torio." And he
dropped the tip of his sword to the ground, as a
sign that the match was over.

"And what would you two do in an even match?" a voice asked, and Bryen strode across the court-yard. "Maldek, is this what you had to show me—the perfect match for the victory games?"

The gambler circled the two panting men, saying, "I want to see you with light swords—or do either of you know how to use a pikestaff? What about wrestling? The local farmers like that—they'll bet everything that's left from their last harvest!"

Zanos stared at the intruder. "Who are you?" he asked, a warning tone in his voice.

Bryen ignored it. "They'll all bet on the big one, of course. You, son," he said to Torio, "you one of Maldek's servants? You got talent there—quick moves. Think you can take this big fellow with a lighter weapon?"

"I'm not a gladiator," Torio replied. "I'm a Reader," he added, thinking that that unfair advantage would surely make him ineligible for what-ever the gambler had in mind.

"All the better! Inner sight against brute strength —the crowd will love it! Maldek, can I take these men with me, to supervise their training? There's only a few days left—I have to decide how to use them to best advantage before I put out the word—"

"Stop!" ordered Zanos. "I spent most of my life fighting in the arena—and I'm not going back to it to line the pockets of another gambler!"

"Oh, you'll be paid!" said Bryen. "Both of you— you just do what I tell you, and we'll line *all* our pockets!"

He started to turn back to Maldek, assuming that everything was settled with Zanos and Torio, but Zanos had fought too long for the right to

control his own life. He grasped the man's arm
and pulled him back around, saying, "Maldek is
not *our* master. No man is. I told you I will never
again kill as an exhibit for other people's pleasure!
Torio?"

"I certainly won't," the Reader said.

"So we are agreed," said Zanos, squeezing Bryen's
arm for emphasis—and lifting it enough that his
eyes fell on the half-grown hand.

Torio felt astonishment stab through Zanos as
he looked from the hand to Bryen's face—to the
fiery red hair with a sprinkling of white at the
temples, the blue eyes. Torio could see the resem-
blance in the square jaw and the shape of the
nose, but Bryen's face had a hardness Zanos' lacked,
even though both men had known a lifetime of
harsh survival.

For a long moment, Zanos only stared. Then,
"Bryen?" he whispered. The gambler only stared
at him. "Bryen—don't you know me? I've come all
the way from Tiberium looking for you . . . my
brother."

NonReader, nonAdept, Bryen had no disciplines
at all to hide his feelings. His utter amazement
washed over Torio in a chill wave. "Zanos? Little
brother?"

The term was absurd—for although Zanos was
hardly a handspan taller than Bryen, he was so
broad and strong from years of training that he
appeared three times his brother's size.

Bryen laughed. "You are! Zanos, I thought I'd
never see you again!" His startlement warmed into
family feeling as the two men hugged, pounding
one another on the back, Zanos almost crushing
Bryen in his enthusiasm.

"I didn't know if you'd even survived!" said Zanos. "I've wanted to come back—but it took me so many years to earn my freedom. . . . And what about you? You look well. Are you married? My wife's here with me—you have to meet her—and my friends, Torio here and—"

As he turned to introduce them, Zanos' eyes fell on Maldek, who was standing back, watching the reunion in open amusement.

Zanos stopped, then said, "You found him for me, didn't you, Maldek?"

"I found him," the sorcerer assented.

"And restored his hand?" The gladiator shook his head slowly. "I still don't know what to think about you—but this time you have my thanks."

This reunion, however, was less sweet than Astra's with her mother. But it was happy enough for the next few hours, as Zanos introduced his brother to the rest of their group, told his story and Astra's, and listened to Bryen's tale of survival.

When the slaver ship departed, Bryen had been left among the dead and dying. The village healer had been slaughtered, so there was no help but what they could do for one another. A man with a gut wound tied a rope around the end of the boy's arm so he would not bleed to death, and together they somehow got another man and a woman into a fishing boat and set out for the next village.

But by dawn all three of Bryen's companions were dead of their wounds. The boy passed out, and the boat drifted aimlessly until other fishermen found it.

They took Bryen to their healer, who saved his life, but only a Master Sorcerer could restore his hand.

"Why wasn't that done?" demanded Zanos. "The Lord of the Land in our day was good and kind—"

"And old," said Bryen. "Oh, he lived for over ten years after you were captured, but his powers were waning. Maldek, his son, was sent to apprentice in Meliard, far to the north, for he was hardly older than I was, and not come into his full powers. We paid so little attention to anything but fishing in our home village—I found in the City that Madura was at war! The fleet was defending the river here; that's why the slavers found it so easy to prey on the southern coast.

"The Lord of the Land granted me audience when he heard my story—but only to tell me no, he couldn't use his strength to heal half-grown boys when he had to keep grown men strong for his army. He promised to heal me as soon as I was full-grown." Bryen snorted derisively. "So much for the promises of the Lord of the Land!"

"The war went on for many years," said Cassandra. "Surely you can understand the difficult decisions he had to make about how best to defend his people. All those years, Bryen, our climate remained mild, our crops and flocks healthy."

"Maybe, but in the City I learned to take care of myself. A man named Graorn took me in, and set me to collecting rents from his tenants. He had a hook made for my missing hand—and I was starting to get big enough that the welchers handed over what they owed when I shoved it in their faces.

"By the time I was old enough to go into the army, I'd seen too many soldiers go out there and almost die, and be healed, and almost die again, and be healed—the second or third time lots of 'em deserted, and hid out in the City. So I just didn't go to get my hand put back."

"Then how can you blame the Lord of the Land for not keeping his promise?" Zanos asked.

"Once the war was over, I went to the castle!" Bryen flared. "That was after Maldek came home. With his powers, it was over fast—and I went to the castle and couldn't even get in! For the next few years, everyone said Maldek was really running things—but mostly life was all right until the old lord died. Then—"

"Yes—we've seen," said Zanos.

"But Maldek seems to be learning from his mistakes," put in Melissa.

"Don't bet on it!" said Bryen. "They say nobody's ever had as much power as Maldek has—so who's gonna stop him from doing whatever he wants?"

"Himself," Melissa answered. "Bryen, he healed you, and reunited you with your brother. He found Astra's mother for her. Can't you see what's happening? He's been so isolated by his power, and by the fear he has generated in his people . . . he's so lonely."

"Lonely!" Dirdra snorted. "He can take anyone he wants!"

"He can by force," agreed Melissa, "but you of all people know that he has found no satisfaction in that."

"So he simply forces people in other ways!" the Maduran woman retorted. "Are you all such fools, to be taken in by his supposed reform?"

"Dirdra, shouldn't we give him the benefit of the doubt?" asked Astra. "Maldek did not have to find my mother. I'd never have known she was in Madura."

"Did you never wonder how he *knew* your mother had left the Aventine Empire?" Dirdra asked. "Astra, he spies on our minds—and you Readers can't even tell he's doing it!"

"That's true," said Torio. "At least while we were on the way here, I felt Maldek's mind searching several times—didn't you, Astra, Melissa?"

Astra nodded. But Melissa said, "Yes—but he was testing us then. He found that we were all friends, and nothing he sent against us could defeat us when we worked together."

"He's clumsy," Zanos put in. "Let's suppose Melissa's right, and we came along just at the time when Maldek had realized that forcing people to do his will wasn't satisfying. Maye he really *is* trying to make friends with us—but all he can think to do is find out what we're looking for, and give it to us."

"He's trying to buy your friendship," said Dirdra.

"He'll learn that only friendship gains friendship," said Melissa. "Astra is right. We ought to assume that Maldek means well until he proves otherwise."

Torio remained quiet through the exchange, for Dirdra expressed his feelings quite well, and he didn't want to fight with Melissa.

She, however, knew what was on his mind, and confronted him after supper that night. "Why didn't you say what you thought this afternoon?"

"What do you mean?"

"Torio, you may be able to hide your precise thoughts from me, but your feelings are on Dirdra's side, against Maldek."

"And why are you so much *for* him?" Torio asked. "Read what his people think about him—how they hid when we went into town, how Bryen distrusted his motives. What's wrong with you, Melissa? Can't you see that he's putting on an act?"

"No, I *don't* see that!" she exploded. "Why would he bother? Torio, the man is putting forth every effort to make up for what he did to us. He's starting work at healing Kwinn in the morning. Maybe Dirdra will come to see that he's trying—"

They were climbing the staircase leading to the upper hallway where their rooms were. From Zanos and Astra's room came a sudden shout that stopped them in their tracks: "No! By Mawort, even if you *are* my brother, I'll never again kill for sport!"

"But the *money*, Zanos—"

"Money? Is that all you think of, Bryen?"

"Money is power—if you don't have any other kind. And even Maldek needs money."

"Zanos, please—calm down," came Astra's voice.

"When my own brother wants to put me back in the arena? Bryen, you make your living out of other men's pain! Don't think I don't understand—that's how I bought my way out of slavery, and won the money to get out of the empire." He let out a bitter laugh. "Only to lose it to a cheating, power-hungry gambler just like you!"

The door to the gladiator's room slammed against the wall as Zanos burst out. He rushed by Torio and Melissa without even seeing them, Bryen following at a discreet distance.

Torio had seen Zanos do this before. Trained to violence, he had taught himself to walk away from

a brewing fight before he hurt someone. Bryen
didn't know the risk he took by pursuing him.

But Astra did—and her mother Read her fear
and exclaimed, "What kind of man have you married, Astra? How could a Reader live daily with
such violence? And he has taught you to carry a
sword—"

"Mother, I love Zanos. He won't hurt Bryen—
that's why he walked away."

"But he's such a . . . brute. Oh, my daughter, if
only I could have been there to guide you—"

"You broke your oath as much as I did mine!"
said Astra. "Don't you talk about guiding me—at
least I *knew* about the corruption in the Academy
system before I deserted it. Portia attacked me
because I knew too much—because of this wild
Reading talent I inherited from you and my father. Did it ever occur to you that the Academy
rules which prevent Master Readers from having
children are there to save children from growing
up as I did, unable to control? It's a wonder I
didn't go mad, and end my life at Gaeta with the
healers tying knots in my mind!"

"So you chose to have your children with that—
that animal?"

"Zanos is a good man—how can you call yourself a Reader and not recognize that?" And Astra
also burst from the room, sailing past Torio and
Melissa, who stared at each other and realized—

"He's got us divided!" exclaimed Torio. "Maldek
could not defeat us as a group—but he now has us
separated, so he can—" Dread suspicion directed
his Reading to the end of the hall. "Where's
Dirdra?"

Only Kwinn was in Dirdra's room, curled up on

the end of the bed, sound asleep. An Adept-induced sleep, obviously, or he would never have allowed Dirdra to leave him alone.

And in Maldek's throne room, Dirdra stood before the Master Sorcerer, who was telling her, "I am truly sorry that I cannot restore Kwinn exactly as he was before—but I know you will teach him to be a good man, and love him as much as you always did."

She regarded him with suspicion as she agreed, "That is true."

"Dirdra, I am asking your forgiveness."

Torio and Melissa took each other's hands, not daring to make a mental comment or even let their feelings surface lest Maldek Read them spying. Could Melissa be right? This was one time Torio would be glad to be proved wrong.

"When I see my brother restored to the man he was—and when in his eyes I see a man's intelligence—then, Master, I will forgive you with all my heart," Dirdra said with her customary dignity.

Maldek smiled his most charming smile, stood, and descended the steps from his throne. He came to Dirdra—too close, daring her to retreat. She stood her ground, and he let his overpowering maleness overshadow her as he said, "I will be happy to accept it then. In the meantime, you may have friends, Dirdra, but in one way you are as lonely as I am—as Kwinn was for you while you were gone."

He looked down into her eyes. "I kept him with me as a reminder of you—your image was the one thing always clear in his mind." He put his hands on her shoulders, ignoring the slight increase in the stiffness of her posture. "I missed you, Dirdra."

He bent his head, kissing her unyielding lips.
Dirdra was not thinking at all, fearing anything
that escaped her control would trigger Maldek's
anger and end her hopes for Kwinn. Maldek must
have known what she was doing, but he continued
gently kissing her cheeks, her eyelids. "You have
no need to fear me. I wouldn't hurt you. Let me
share with you, Dirdra. Think of what pleasure a
Master Sorcerer can provide—"

"Please, Master, do not touch me further," Dirdra
said quietly, firmly.

He lifted his head, but did not take his hands
from her shoulders. "Dirdra, you are mine. You
are my subject, and I can do with you what I
will—but instead I offer you freely—"

"Master, you do not offer freely the chance to
refuse you."

Maldek's eyes glinted coldly. "It is irrational for
you to refuse me. Rokannia, a Master Sorceress, is
on the sea, bound for Madura. When she arrives,
she will once again ask of me as a favor what you
will not take freely given!"

"Rokannia wants your child, not you," said
Dirdra. "She would raise that child to your strength
without your cruelty. Together they would free
the Western Isle of your tyranny—perhaps Madura,
too, for it would be your child's inheritance."

Her green eyes stared up at him defiantly. "Do
you think that people without the inner sight have
no minds? You want me only because I refuse
you. Would that I had given in at the very
beginning—you would have discarded me without
harming my brother."

"And I shall have you now, and discard you as I
please—"

//Zanos! Astra! Cassandra!// Torio broadcast at the strongest intensity. //Maldek is threatening Dirdra!//

He and Melissa ran toward the throne room, Gray surging ahead of them. The guards barred their way, but Melissa had the power to make them sleep. As they collapsed, sliding down the wall, Torio flung the door open.

"Where are your fine promises and good intentions now, Maldek?" he demanded.

"Spying on me, Torio?" asked the sorcerer conversationally.

"Merely making certain of Dirdra's safety. We share a bond of friendship."

Zanos arrived, trailed by Bryen, while Cassandra met her daughter at the juncture of the passageways, and the two women marched defiantly into the throne room together.

"Torio was right!" said Melissa. "You haven't changed, Maldek—you just wanted us to think you had."

"When you found my brother," said Zanos, "you knew he was the kind of man who would bring dissension into our group."

"The gods forgive me," added Cassandra, "but you must have brought me here knowing that I would not approve of my daughter's choice of husband, and might drive them apart. Astra, I am sorry. I have seen how much Zanos loves you, and what else matters?"

"Nothing," replied Astra, linking arms with her mother. "Dirdra—come and join us. We are family— as long as we remain together, Maldek cannot harm us."

Dirdra took Astra's other arm. Torio and Melissa took their places, and Zanos and Bryen forged the link on the other side of Cassandra.

The Master Sorcerer laughed. "I could kill you all, right there where you stand!"

"You can kill us," said Melissa, "but you cannot bend us to your will. I was wrong about you, Maldek. You haven't yet learned that kindness makes friends as close as brothers, but threats create only frightened enemies."

"Indeed? You want to be brothers? Do you want Bryen as your brother—gambler, extortionist, exploiter of other men's pain? You didn't like what you found very much, did you, Zanos?"

"He is my brother," Zanos insisted. "We were separated as boys, so we don't know one another very well yet—but we will come to understand each other."

"You five who came so far together—Zanos, Astra, Torio, Melissa, Dirdra—do you feel like brothers and sisters? Do you really know one another any better than you do Bryen and Cassandra?"

"After what you put us through?" asked Torio. "I would trust any of my friends with my life— and have done so."

"But . . . could they trust you?" asked Maldek with a malicious smile.

"Of course," said Zanos. "We have all trusted Torio with our lives."

"Not knowing what you risked!" Maldek told them. "Do you know why he is so afraid of wielding power? Do you know what Torio did to his *own* brother?"

Melissa turned. "Torio? You never told me you had a brother."

"He died," Torio replied. "I hardly remember

him—we were just little boys—I couldn't have been more than four years old. Before any of my Reading powers began to develop."

"But you had power, Torio," said Maldek. "You were blind—and so your mother set you over your brother, even though he was older. He had to obey your every whim, remember?"

"No," Torio said truthfully, "I *don't* remember. I can hardly recall anything before Master Lenardo discovered that I was a Reader and took me to the Academy at Adigia."

"Then remember *now*!" said Maldek—and suddenly Torio and all the other Readers there were enveloped helplessly in nightmare.

It was his dream!

The moment it began he recognized it, although every time he woke from it he found it gone beyond recall.

He was a child, small and helpless in a world where everyone else strode freely, but he had to feel his way unless someone led him by the hand.

Having never seen, he did not understand the power sighted people had—only that he bumped into things other people miraculously knew were there, and that he could not find his way outside the small apartment where he lived with his father, mother, and brother Detrus.

Only in their home was his world safe and warm; there he was held and fed and loved. But Detrus had to take care of him when both their parents were working—and Detrus would rather play with the other boys than nursemaid his blind brother.

One day Detrus took him outside and left him sitting against a wall while he played with the other boys.

Out of nothingness came the sound of footsteps—
but not human steps. Something with claws click-
ing on the cobbles!

He smelled a strange odor—it came closer and
he shrank back against the wall. Icy wetness nudged
his neck—a slavering beast began licking his face—

He screamed!

The thing barked, hot breath with the odor of
garbage in his face—

And his brother and his friends came running—
not to rescue him, but to howl with laughter!

That evening, clutching his mother as if he would
never let go, Torio begged, "Don' lee me with
Detrus no more, Mama! It was a monster! It wanted
to eat me up!"

"It was just a *dog*!" Detrus explained. "It wouldn't
of hurt Torio—just washed his face for him." He
laughed.

But it wasn't funny to their mother.

"Torio can't help being blind," she reminded
Detrus. "You know your father and I both have to
work. You have to take care of your brother—an'
no more leaving him alone, in the house or
outside!"

"But Mama—" Detrus protested.

"No!" she told him. "You stay inside and play
Torio's games! You feed him when he's hungry.
If he wants to go outside, you hold him by the
hand, and take him where he wants to go. And
Torio—if Detrus ever scares you again, you let me
know!"

For the first time in his life, a feeling of power
surged through Torio.

Then it was another afternoon, after lunch. He
made Detrus play the word-guessing game he hated

because Torio, although two years younger, was better at it than he was. But "I'll tell Mama" was all Torio had to threaten to get what he wanted.

"That's a dumb game!" said Detrus after Torio won another round. "Words are for girls and blind kids. You can't do nothin' fun, Torio."

"What do you wanna do?" Torio asked, feeling magnanimous. "We could sing songs."

"That's for *little* kids!"

"You could tell me a story."

"I don't know any stories."

"Yes you do. Tell me about the wild boy raised by the wolves." In Torio's mind, a wolf must be much like the dog that had come out of nowhere and terrified him.

But he knew it was a favorite story with Detrus, who had actually seen the wild boy in a cage when the carnival came through their town last summer. In fact, Detrus had been talking about the wild boy recently because they had heard that the carnival was in one of the nearby towns, and might be coming back to their town soon.

Detrus told the story, getting into the spirit as he described the boy's shaggy hair and long, sharp teeth, growling in imitation of the way he had growled at the crowd.

"And then, when fat Orfio got real close and tried to touch him," Detrus ended in a fit of giggles, "he lifted his leg just like a dog and peed right out of the cage on him!"

Torio giggled, too, in boyish comradeship at sharing a story their mother would never have approved of.

Just then running footsteps pounded down the

street outside. "Carnival's coming! Carnival's coming!" shouted boys' voices.

Someone hammered on the door. "Detrus! Hey—Detrus! Come on! Let's see if they've still got the wild boy!"

Torio recognized Orfio's voice. "Come *on*, Detrus! We're gonna miss it! I'm gonna get that wild boy—I got a good sharp stick to jab 'im with!"

"Torio—you stay here," ordered Detrus. "I'm only gonna go an' see the wild boy, and then I'll be right back—all right?"

"No!" said Torio. "No, Detrus! Mama said you gotta stay here with me!"

"Not on carnival day! Torio—you don't tell her, and I'll bring you a sugar sop."

"Where you gonna get a sugar sop?" demanded Torio. "You're lying, Detrus! I'll tell Mama!"

"I'll pinch you!" Detrus said angrily, suiting action to words.

"I'll tell Mama!" Torio screamed the louder.

"I'll put you outside where the dogs'll eat you up!" Detrus threatened.

"An' Mama'll punish you!" Torio retorted, feeling his power in the fact that Detrus remained there arguing instead of just running off.

That fact gave him courage.

"Take me along."

"I can't do that! You'd get lost."

"Not if you hold my hand like Mama said. I wanna go to the carnival, Detrus. You take me!" said Torio, stomping his foot for emphasis.

By the time they were at the end of their street, Torio regretted his hasty decision.

They got into a jostling crowd, and Torio was

lost already. If Detrus let go of his hand, he'd never find his way home!

He stopped, digging in his heels. "Detrus, I wanna go home!"

"No! You wanted to come along, now you come!" said Detrus. "Hurry *up*, Torio! We'll miss the parade!"

Detrus gave a jerk to Torio's hand, and the blind boy stumbled after him, terror building. Up ahead there were rumbling noises, and roars and growls along with the stink of wild beasts—real wild beasts, not neighborhood dogs and cats!

"I wanna go home!" Torio screamed the louder, but Detrus dragged him along, in among packed bodies, bumping into people, worming their way through to where Detrus could see the passing wagons.

"There's the wild boy!" Detrus shouted. "Come on, Torio—Orfio's tryin' a catch up—I wanna see if he sticks him!"

"I wanna go home!" Torio cried again as Detrus hauled him along. Suddenly he dug in his heels, grabbed Detrus' hand in both of his, and swung his brother away from the direction he was headed. "You gotta do what *I* want, Detrus! I wanna go *home!*"

Torio knew nothing of where they were except that they had broken through the crowd that he could still hear, and all around them were loud rumbles of heavy animal wagons with their growling beasts and sharp ammonia stinks.

He swung Detrus in the direction he thought they had come from.

Detrus stumbled—and his hand slipped out of Torio's!

"Detrus!" Torio screamed.

Other voices in the crowd began to scream.

"Look out!"

"Watch out for the boys!"

Horses neighed in terror.

Fear stench rose all around.

The rumble grew louder, shaking the ground as Torio groped wildly for Detrus—

Heard his brother's scream—

Heard horses scream again—

Heard people screaming all around—

Smelled—blood!

In Maldek's throne room, Torio stood sweating and shaking as he did when he awoke from that same nightmare. Now he knew why he could never remember it.

Tears streaking his face, he sank to his knees, whispering, "Now you know—now we all know. I'm responsible. I killed my brother."

Chapter Seven

*F*rom all around the throne room, waves of anger washed through Torio's battered mind.

Overpowering surges of guilt ripped through him as he knelt, exposed, before the people who had been his friends. Shielding from their fury, he withdrew into himself, as blind and helpless as he had been as a small boy.

Claws clicked on the stone floor, and Gray licked his face, nudging him under the chin, offering unquestioning comfort even though the dog had Read Torio's experience along with all the other Readers.

Then a gentle hand touched his shoulder. "Torio." It was Dirdra's voice. "Don't let Maldek do this to you."

"You don't understand," he said wretchedly. "You couldn't Read—" He threw his arms around Gray, not caring that the dog still loved him only because it couldn't comprehend the enormity of his guilt.

"*I* could Read it," said Melissa, kneeling on

Torio's other side and putting her arms around
him. "Torio—do you think we would blame you
for an accident? You were too young even to
understand what was happening! Torio?"

He could not respond, keeping his face buried
against Gray, his mind firmly closed. Melissa's pity
was even worse than her anger of the moment
before.

Then strong hands grasped his upper arms.
"Stand up!" said Zanos, lifting him to his feet.
"Torio—*Read*! For Hesta's sake—we're angry at
Maldek, not at you! What kind of evil mind tries
to cast guilt on a man for what happened when he
was a four-year-old child?"

"But it was my fault—" Torio began.

"Nonsense!" declared Zanos. "Have you Read
Bryen blaming me for the loss of his hand? Or me
blaming him for letting me be carried off into
slavery? Or either of us laden with guilt for the
deaths of the rest of our family? By the gods,
Torio, you take responsibility for everything that
happens, as if to make up for that one event that
was *not your fault*."

Hesitantly, Torio allowed himself to Read—and
found that Dirdra, Melissa, and Zanos spoke the
truth. It was not even that his friends forgave
him—they found nothing to forgive!

Unlike his mother.

For the two years he had remained at home
after Detrus' death, Torio had lived with a silent
woman who blamed her crippled son for the death
of her perfect one. She had neither punished nor
neglected him—but she had not loved him. And
Torio's growing powers had only revealed more
and more how much his mother blamed him for

something his young mind had banished from memory.

But he remembered clearly how happy his mother was to be rid of him when then-Magister Lenardo had discovered his potential as a Reader and taken him off to the Academy.

The Readers had taken four boys from six to eight years old out of their town that day. Torio, the youngest, was the only one who did not cry himself to sleep in his strange bed that night ... the only one who did not want to go home again.

What he felt this evening in the throne room of Maldek's castle was the same sense of relief he had known at the Academy, where his teachers had cared only about his Reading potential, and no one had blamed him for anything beyond boyish pranks.

This feeling was even more welcome. His friends *knew*—and they didn't hate him! He Read their love, their caring as they gathered around him, even Bryen and Cassandra joining the circle to put their arms around him, protecting him against the malice of the Master Sorcerer—

Who stood partway up the steps to his throne, watching the scene in growing anger.

Astra turned to him. "We won't let you pull that trick again, Maldek. We have our differences—but you will never again divide us!"

And as if her words were a signal—thunder roared outside, and people began to scream!

They Read outward, to find the city under attack.

Fire rained from the sky. Thunderbolts struck the castle. The forest roared into flame, animals fleeing, leaping into the river and the moat—

"Rokannia!" shouted Maldek.

But there was more than one Adept attacking!

In savage glee, the Readers felt Maldek recognize that the very tricks he had been using on his visitors had been turned against him.

While Maldek had been preoccupied with trying to divide and conquer his guests, Rokannia had taken the opportunity to gather two other Master Sorcerers against him—one of them Borru of Meliard, with whom he had been fostered as a boy.

Torio felt Maldek's shock of recognition—Borru was his mentor, Rokannia his sworn vassal, and Shivahn his neighbor to the northwest, with whom he had an uneasy truce.

//How dare you attack me?// he demanded.

Rokannia answered for them all. //You destroy my people with your demands, Maldek—and your ruin of your own lands is spreading to those of your neighbors on Madura! You are at war with us, whether you declare it or not.//

//Borru,// Maldek appealed, //Master. You taught me to use my powers. How can you turn against me?//

//You have misused your powers, Maldek, against your people, your land. You must be stopped before you destroy everything your father left to you.//

//This is *my* land,// Maldek told them. //I will do with it as I please!//

//No,// said Shivahn, //the land is not yours, nor the people—you are theirs! And your loss of control of the climate has crept year by year into my lands, until my crops fail under early and late frosts, my herds die in the winter storms—and my people suffer hunger! No more, Maldek. You will be stopped, once and for all!//

//Give it up, Maldek,// said Rokannia. //Your powers may be greater than ours individually—but our combined powers are greater than anything you have.//

//You are wrong!// Maldek roared aloud even as he projected the thought. //I know where you are—and I will destroy you!//

And with that he sent a thunderbolt crackling to where Rokannia was hidden in the forest on the other side of the river—for, Torio realized, while Maldek was distracted with the games he was playing with his visitors, the three Master Sorcerers had left Rokannia's ship and traveled inland on the same road Torio and his companions had taken.

Of course—these three had the power to fool Maldek's Readers. They had not even known two other sorcerers were aboard Rokannia's vessel. The ship was still proceeding around the southeast tip of the island, as if to sail up to the City by the river, as expected. No one had reported that it had put people ashore.

Rokannia and her cohorts easily deflected Maldek's first blow and sent their own barrage against the castle, shaking its foundations. But it was built to withstand Adept attack, and nothing happened beyond a loud rattling.

Kwinn, however, wakened in terror and galloped down the stairs squealing, looking for Dirdra. When he found her, he flung his arms around her and buried his face in her skirt to be stroked and comforted.

Outside, local minor Adepts had already put

out the forest fire—but Torio could Read that
such an effort quickly used up their meager powers.

He caught Rokannia Reading him—in fact, Reading the whole group gathered before Maldek. //Join
with us!// she directed. //Maldek has proven himself your enemy—help us to kill him, and you will
have three Master Sorcerers in your debt!//

But it was not their war—at least not yet. Torio
Read the consensus that they protect themselves,
but not attack—a spontaneous response from all
who could Read Rokannía's offer.

"Don't listen to her," warned Maldek. "I will
win. Be my friends, not my enemies! Help me,
and I will reward you well."

He probably Read the skepticism with which
they heard that offer, but again they remained
spontaneously neutral, waiting to see the outcome—
all heartily wishing they were not trapped between
Maldek's evil and the uncertainty of Rokannia and
her friends.

The attacking forces again struck with fire—
Torio had seen this method of attack many times
before. In the City, several neighborhoods blazed
up, people running helplessly, minor Adepts res-
cuing those they could, healers rushing to save
people who had inhaled smoke or been burned.

But then there were no new fires as the three
Master Sorcerers concentrated so hard that they
could not be Read unless one knew where to visualize them—and overhead storm clouds gathered,
black and threatening. As they were creating them
in a cloudless sky, Torio knew they were working
against nature, using a great deal of Adept power.

//You think thunder and lightning will frighten

me?// Maldek demanded sarcastically—but his audience was not listening.

Something more was happening in those clouds—water droplets were being urged together, freezing wind condensing them into ice crystals, larger and larger chunks—

Hail the size of melons began to fall on the City and the castle!

People and animals were struck and killed.

Roofs were pierced—and those which first held gave way under further bombardment and the sheer weight of ice.

Even the castle roof was struck through, great ice balls smashing on the stone floors.

But Maldek grabbed hold of the wind, and sent the hail sheering from the upper atmosphere across the river to strike the people who had created it.

Shivahn moved her attention from forming the hail to melting what Maldek was throwing at them before it could strike.

He focused on her—and the sorceress' heart shuddered and heaved as searing pain clutched at her chest!

Her attention focused on her own body as, shaking, she fought Maldek's squeezing of her heart.

Fortunately for Shivahn, Maldek dared not concentrate for long on just one person—for while his attention was thus engaged, Rokannia and Borru were directing the hailstones to crush his castle walls—stone walls pierced by ice, driven by Adept powers.

The castle shook as the kitchen wing collapsed.

Maldek had to concentrate on melting the ice before it struck—and at the same time protect himself as the three Master Sorcerers launched an attack on his body, trying to stop his heart or paralyze his diaphragm so he could not breathe.

//Fools!// Rokannia stormed at Maldek's visitors. //You are closer than we are! Kill him where he stands before—//

But it was too late. Maldek was calling upon the planes of power—Torio could Read a strange aura of energy around him, protecting, even absorbing the blows the others sent against him, thus increasing its own power.

Astonishment rang from Borru. //Maldek—what are you doing? You cannot control so much power!//

//I am doing what you taught me, Master!// Maldek replied cynically.

//We must stop him *now*!// exclaimed the sorcerer from the far north. //Come—join with me!//

And the three joined hands, Borru reaching for the same source of power Maldek was tapping—but with a difference.

Maldek was using the power as an outer defense. The sorcerer from Meliard merely drew strength into his own body, as if to heal the weakness caused by the use of Adept powers. Thus strengthened, he joined his companions in the attack with powers Torio was only too familiar with.

Searing flames rose all around!

Hot fire of destruction!

The tapestries went up in flames, the paneling, the wooden throne, the rugs—

Kwinn screamed, and Gray yelped in terror.

The doors burst into flame.

The Readers gasped in disbelief as the very stone walls began to burn.

They were trapped!

Even Maldek had to have air to breathe—and the fire was taking all the air!

Torio choked and gasped, trying to Read a way out. There was flame in every direction.

Heat seared his flesh.

Melissa, Zanos, and Astra fought the fire, but succeeded only in creating a flameless circle around them—there was still no way out!

Maldek concentrated—and cold white fire leaped across the river, attacking the circle of sorcerers—

It burned through their nerves, not healing now, but draining them with searing pain until they shriveled, agony traveling up their spines to their brains, roaring through their minds and leaving them dead—empty!

Maldek had won.

But his throne room was surrounded by fire, the walls, the floor, the very air aflame.

Outside, the forest blazed.

The City roared to the heavens!

All the power their own small circle of Adepts could muster could not hold off the conflagration any longer—they were dying.

"Maldek!" Melissa screamed. "Stop the fire! It will kill you, too!"

He Read that it was destroying his castle, his City—and in pure selfishness he once again reached for that cold white flame—

"Not more fire!" cried Torio—

But then he saw what Maldek was doing.

The cold fire attacked the hot—absorbed it! It spread, circling the group of visitors, drawing power from the flames it fed on and leaving only ash in its wake. Cold ash.

Everyone stared, gasping for breath.

Up the walls went the cold white fire, feeding on the hot orange flames, consuming them and leaving refreshing coolness.

Melissa stared at Maldek. "Such power," she whispered. "Blessed gods—he is truly invincible!"

Maldek grinned triumphantly, striding down the barren steps as the fire retreated.

About him was still that aura of cold fire.

"Melissa," Torio warned, "do not touch him! That power is working *through* him!"

"Of course," replied Maldek. "I am its route into this world—only I dare call up so much power. Poor Borru—all he ever tried to teach me was to control, control, never loose the true power of which I am capable. Now he knows, wherever he is, what power he could have had if he hadn't been afraid!"

The Master Sorcerer held out his hands, one to Dirdra, one to Melissa. "All power is mine. Rokannia, Borru, Shivahn—their lands are mine now. And you are mine. I have won the right to you—all of you. Please me, and I will reward you. Displease me—"

He had no need to finish the threat. Neither woman, though, touched him. "You fear me," he said, obviously pleased. "That is wise."

"I do not fear you," said Dirdra. "Nothing has changed. You cannot do anything more to me than you have already done."

"Dirdra is right," said Melissa. "What have you gained, Maldek? More power? You didn't know what to do with what you had. Read what is happening out there—the force you unleashed may put out the fires, but it will not restore the lives of

the people who died. It will not bring the forest
back, fresh and green. Only time will heal those
terrible scars—and even time will not help if you
continue to destroy your land."

Torio recalled his prophecy. "Maldek, your land
is worse off now than before the attack. Your
major trade city lies in ashes. You are your land—do
not think that you have any more power than it
has."

"Do you think your nonsense frightens me,
Torio? *I* decide my fate, not some foolish Reader
who will not even see, let alone learn to use the
other side of his powers. Borru tried to make me
into someone like you—afraid of power—and see
where he lies now. With my powers, I need have
no fear of superstition!"

"Then what," Astra put in, "are you going to do
about the power you have unleashed? Can you
control what it is doing now, Maldek?"

Everyone Read with her—and found the cold
white energy drawing back toward the castle. All
the fires were out—but people lay dead or dying
. . . and as it retreated, the cold fire, having consumed its prime target, now sucked the life from
anyone it met who could not shield.

Those with either Reading or Adept power managed to fight it off—but they saw friends and
family drained of life in its wake, and screams of
renewed agony followed upon the sobs of the
already grief-stricken.

"No!" exclaimed Maldek—and for the first time
Torio Read genuine fear grasp at the man's mind.

But the Master Sorcerer wasted no time on his
apprehensions—he reached out with his powerful

mind, drawing the circle of cold fire back toward the castle, to himself, so that he could banish it—

Where freezing emptiness had been, cold flames flickered and leaped, eluding Maldek's attempts to direct the fire—it seared through him, cold and deadly, tapping the power of its own plane to renew its strength.

With a mighty effort of will, Maldek forced the white fire to retreat to the castle—where it broke forth in even greater force!

Where orange heat had consumed before, now unyielding cold ravaged through the castle—

Torio Read what was happening:

Maldek was the conduit for this force from another plane of existence.

The farther it ranged from its link with its own world, the weaker it became, and the more easily he could control it.

But when he drew it toward himself, to force it back onto its own plane, it renewed itself by contact with its origins, and could resist him!

Zanos, Melissa, and Astra automatically joined their efforts to Maldek's—but their powers were nothing compared to his, and they made no perceptible impact.

The cold energy leaped about the castle—striking the living, drawing their life. Many of Maldek's servants had powers. They resisted, but those who had no defenses succumbed without even knowing what had struck them—and with every life, the draining force grew hungrier.

"Dirdra!" Torio shouted. "Take Kwinn and Bryen and—"

Then he realized that they were surrounded—as

Maldek closed the circle of energy, it had to travel over, past, or through all of them!

"Protect them!" he directed, and they shoved the three with no powers to the center of their circle, Torio, Melissa, Astra, Zanos, and Cassandra joining hands around them. Gray patrolled the outside of their circle as Maldek stood on the steps to his throne—now a pile of ashes—intent on conquering that cold energy as he had conquered every other opponent in his life.

As he drew the cold fire toward himself, it flicked over the circle of portectors. Torio felt it tingle through his nerves, far stronger than when it was used for healing. He shivered as it tried to draw the warmth from him—but instinctively, without knowing how he did it, he let it flow through him without effect.

So did Melissa, Zanos, Astra, Cassandra—and even Gray.

But Dirdra could not let it flow, nor Kwinn nor Bryen—in them, the cold drained, drained—

"Maldek—stop it!" shouted Melissa.

He did not reply—there *was* no possible reply! He was struggling with all his might. Torio Read his dominant emotion: not fear, but utter astonishment.

Never since he had come into the full flush of his powers had Maldek met a force he could not conquer!

The more Maldek struggled, the stronger the unleashed force became. Never before had the Master Sorcerer allowed it to reach beyond his touch—and now it sought mindlessly the freedom it had briefly known, pure power seeking to consume—

It broke free!

The Adepts were blank to Reading as they struggled to aid Maldek—but their abilities were nothing to his, and he could not control the force he had set loose.

Rampaging now, it seemed a living thing escaped from long imprisonment—

But it was *not* a reasoning thing.

There was no appeal to it, any more than one could reason with a flood or an earthquake.

The consuming energy burned Maldek with cold fire as it poured forth from his outstretched arms, then from every pore of his body, surging outward, seeking life, sucking energy out of the very stone.

Again the wave of life-sapping power washed through the circle of Readers and Adepts—but this time they could not protect Dirdra, Kwinn, Bryen. Already weakened, they were sucked dry, left lifeless husks . . . even the warmth was gone from their bodies, and they were left frozen.

The cold spread and spread, drawing life and warmth from everything it touched, feeding itself and growing stronger.

Shaking with the blasts of cold air, Torio turned from the now useless circle. Gray leaned up against him, seeking to share warmth, while Melissa got up from Reading the corpses of their friends, tears freezing on her lashes before they could fall. She buried her hands in Gray's fur, also seeking warmth.

Torio's breath was white smoke as he shouted, "Maldek, it's destroying your land! It will kill your people, and the very earth itself! Let go, Maldek! Cut it off from its source!"

"How?" demanded the sorcerer, no longer seeming to stand there of his own volition, but to be suspended by the force flowing through his body.

"*You* are the avenue of power," Torio explained. "Let go, Maldek—save what is left of your land!"

And the Master Sorcerer, realizing that the only way to cut off that draining power was to destroy its means of access, knew: he had to die.

"No!" he howled.

The numbing cold crept up Torio's legs, and bit at his fingers. "You have no choice!" he shouted. "It will take you after it has taken everything else!"

Cassandra fell to her knees, arms wrapped around herself, cold seeping toward her vital organs.

"No! I will control it!" Maldek insisted, although he had no strength left.

"It's *using* you!" Torio insisted. "The only way to control it is to shut it off! Maldek—it's going to *take* your life—let it go *now*, and save everyone left alive!"

Zanos and Astra huddled together, slumping to the floor as the sleep before death took them over.

"Maldek, our friends are dying!" said Melissa. "It will kill you after it's drained everything else. Let go now, while there is some hope for your land!"

But Maldek would not listen.

Torio felt Melissa Reading him, Cassandra, Zanos, and Astra—all were dying. Gray dropped to the frozen floor, frost on his coat, and Torio could not keep his feet, could not even feel them.

But Melissa did not fall. Instead she stumbled toward Maldek, pleading, "You must die for your land, Maldek—to live forever in the land itself and the memory of your sacrifice."

She reached toward him.

"No! Melissa—no!" Torio tried to shout, but his sluggish body produced no more than a choked gasp as he launched himself toward her. His legs would not obey him.

Melissa took one of Maldek's outstretched hands. "Let me help you," she said, her healer's instinct reaching to aid him through the transition—

But the moment she touched him, the cold fire poured through her body as it did his!

Reading, Torio knew faster than thought what Melissa would do. "No! No! Let go!" he screamed, panic forcing his sluggish blood to pound through his arteries.

This time he gained his feet, stumbled forward, reaching for Melissa to break the contact—

He felt her surprise, her confusion, her fear—

"Torio—oh!" she shouted, the name broken off bluntly. Then the set of her mind turned to total determination.

The devouring force cut off, as sharply as if sliced with a sword.

Maldek fell backward, released, a stringless marionette.

And Melissa, loosed from his grip, dropped lifeless into Torio's outstretched arms.

Chapter Eight

$\mathcal{T}$ime was suspended as Torio held Melissa's body, shivering with cold and shock. Then slowly, instinctively, he Read around them.

Maldek was alive ... barely. Not only was he unconscious, but he did not Read like a Reader—there was no trace of his special powers.

Zanos and Astra lived, as did Cassandra. Gray struggled to crawl toward Torio, whining.

Dirdra and Kwinn lay dead in one another's arms, Bryen fallen over them.

And Torio held Melissa's lifeless body, too deep into shock for tears.

He could not have said how long he sat on the cold stone steps to the burned-out throne, frost settling onto his hair, onto Melissa ... but finally Gray nudged him, transmitting urgency as he butted Torio with his great head, over and over.

Torio looked up—and realized that although the draining force was gone, the castle was colder than any winter he had ever known. If something

was not done soon, those who now only slept
would slip across into death.

More deaths to my account, he thought. There had
to be *something* he could do.

Even if he had had Adept powers, he could not
have started a fire—there was nothing left to burn!

Except—

Their clothing had escaped. In fighting the fire
off their bodies, they had protected that as well.

Laying Melissa down tenderly, Torio took Gray
over to Zanos and Astra, making the dog lie down
against them. Then he moved Cassandra next to
her daughter, and finally dragged Maldek down
off the steps—only because any body warmth he
might have left could serve to keep Torio's friends
alive.

Feeling like a grave robber, he forced himself to
strip the outer garments off Dirdra and Bryen
and placed them in the grate in the fireplace—but
there was nothing with which to strike a light.

Fires here were started by people with Adept
powers, of which Torio had none.

The numbing cold was making it difficult to
think. They had not brought a tinderbox on their
journey, for Zanos, Astra, and Melissa could all
start fires. But he could Read no lighted torch, no
glowing coal in the castle. All had been victim to
the energy-draining power Maldek had loosed upon
his land.

Torio realized he was going to die.

Then he would be with Melissa.

Gray let out a mournful howl—right into Zanos'
ear.

The gladiator came to sluggish wakefulness, looking around—but it was pitch-black in the window-

less throne room. It took him long moments to begin to Read—and then he was as awake as possible in the unremitting cold. "Torio—what?"

"Can you . . . light the fire?" Torio forced out.

Zanos struggled to sit up, could not stand. Torio could feel his deep longing to sink back to sleep, but Zanos had the concentration of an athlete. He forced himself to focus. Finally a small flame flickered in the bunched-up cloth.

Zanos crawled to the fire and tried to warm his hands. "We'll need more than this," he said. "I've never been so cold in my life!"

"I don't know if there's anything left," Torio said dully.

"You're a better Reader than I am," said Zanos. "You tell me where to find fuel, and I'll get it."

There were some charred remains of the doors to the throne room. A wooden chest in the hallway had been scorched but not consumed, and the two men dragged that in and broke it up.

Soon they had a small semicircle of warmth right around the fire—but ever at their backs hovered the implacable cold.

"We'd better wake everyone," said Zanos. "They could die in their sleep before it's warm enough in here to protect them."

When her husband touched her on the forehead, Astra's eyes fluttered open. She smiled weakly at him, then sat up and began to examine her mother. "Torio—"

"I Read it," he replied. "Her hands and feet are frozen. She cannot recover without healing."

"I'll try," said Astra—but her own powers were so drained that she could not produce the healing fire to restore Cassandra. "We need Melissa," she whispered. But then she looked toward Maldek. "He has the power—"

"Had," said Torio. "Read him, Astra. He is more in need of healing than your mother—his whole body has been burned, inside and out. He simply refuses to die."

"Zanos," Astra appealed. "Please help me!"

Cassandra's heart rate slowed drastically. "No!" exclaimed Astra. "Mother, I've just found you. We've lost Zanos' brother. Don't you leave us, too!"

But Cassandra's life was fading.

Torio was used to Adepts handling such situations—but he had had emergency training in his last years at Adigia, before there *were* Adepts to help with healing. Any boy old enough to participate in battle was taught life-saving techniques, including how to start a heart that had stopped with shock.

So as Cassandra's heart stuttered to a halt, he knelt over her and began to press sharply on her breastbone.

"No," said Zanos. "I have enough strength for that." And as Torio sat back, he started Cassandra's heart beating again at a steady rate. Soon it continued on its own. "Other healers must have survived," Zanos said. "Astra, if we can keep her alive, as cold as it is her flesh will not turn putrid before someone can heal her. You will—"

"Zanos, I'm not half the healer Melissa is—was. Nor were the healers we met in the City infirmary. Oh, blessed gods, I know enough of healing to know that her blood will clot where her flesh is frozen—and eventually a clot will hit her heart or her brain—"

"Hush," said Zanos, taking his trembling wife into his arms. "Astra—we've come this far together. We'll heal Cassandra, or find someone who can."

It wouldn't be Maldek, Torio knew. The Master Sorcerer still showed no signs of consciousness— and he had not done what any wounded Adept did automatically: he had not gone into healing sleep. Probably he would die.

Good riddance, Torio thought, stroking Gray and trying not to think of Melissa as Zanos and Astra comforted one another. Astra was murmuring words of sympathy to her husband now about his brother, as both wept shamelessly.

Not to intrude on their privacy, Torio Read elsewhere—and could not escape the fact that Melissa's body lay at the foot of the steps, ice starting to creep—

It was not yet frozen inside! As he Read it, he remembered that moment when she had grasped Maldek's hand, become a conduit herself for the terrible force—and her shock, surprise, fear—!

Blessed gods! Melissa never feared death. She had cried out to him—to say goodbye? To call him into death with her?

No—Melissa was a giver of life, not a taker.

But her cry had been an appeal, not a leave-taking. She had called on him for help—and he had let her die! Just as he had let Detrus die—!

It was not Melissa's time to die. He suddenly knew that as positively as he knew any of his other prophecies. And if it was not yet her time—

What if she is lost among the planes of existence?

"Zanos! Astra!" Torio exclaimed. "We must have a healer—and Melissa needs my help!"

"What?" Zanos asked in confusion.

"Make Melissa's body live!" he said. "You can do it—make her heart beat. Make her breathe!"

"Torio!" exclaimed Astra. "Have you gone mad? That is what Maldek did to create orbu. You do not want Melissa condemned to that!"

"I'll bring her back!" he said. "She died Maldek's death, not her own! That's what the prophecy meant, I'm certain of it. It is not Melissa's time to die. I'll go among the planes of existence and find her—unite her spirit with her body."

"Torio," said Astra, "no one has ever done that."

"Yes they have!" he insisted. "*I* did it—along with other Readers and Adepts. We brought Master Clement back when he was lost on the planes of existence. Zanos, Astra—Melissa may be lost the same way. Please—bring her body back for me!"

Zanos and Astra stared at one another. "I don't think we have the power—" Zanos began.

"All you have to do is start her heart, keep her breathing. *Please!*"

"Torio," said Astra, "what if you are wrong? No one has ever found the plane of the dead . . . and returned."

"Astra, I have to try. You'd do it for Zanos, wouldn't you?"

She looked at her husband, and Torio Read the agreement pass between them.

Carefully, they brought Melissa's body over to the fire. In the freezing temperatures, it had not begun to decompose. Her extremities were frozen—but if Torio was right Melissa would be able to heal herself, and then Cassandra, of any damage.

Together, Zanos and Astra had the strength to start Melissa's heart, to make her lungs expand

and contract—but unlike Cassandra's, Melissa's body did not take up the established rhythms on its own. They did not know Maldek's secret for making orbu do so.

At least, if Torio failed, Melissa's body would not be condemned to that half-life.

He lay down carefully before the fire, Gray curling up protectively against him as if the dog somehow understood that his master's body required protection.

Then Torio was out of his body, light and free as always—free of the painful, penetrating cold.

For a moment he looked down at himself, then at Melissa. She appeared to be asleep; only a Reader could tell that she was dead.

But now . . . how was he to find her spirit?

There were many planes of existence. What Readers called the "plane of privacy" was undoubtedly a different place every time one went there—or perhaps a different place for each person, since one had to lead the other when two Readers sought a private conversation, and no other Reader could follow at a later time.

The plane of privacy was empty. Readers were warned not to come here alone, for the emptiness could drag at one's being just as the cold fire had sucked up energy—

At the thought, Torio was suddenly aware of—

It was a trace of that cold fire! Dead now, cut off from its source, it had nonetheless left its impression.

Torio followed it, and dared at its core to tilt into another plane—where again he found that slight trace of the dissipated power.

Never had Torio been more than two planes of

existence from his physical self. It was possible to be lost even on the plane of privacy—but he could not stop now!

Again he followed the trace of dead energy, and found himself under a night sky filled with stars.

No—not under—in the middle of. He was out in the midst of space, stars off in every direction to the very edges of the universe.

How marvelous to remain suspended here forever, reveling in such beauty—

But Melissa was not here. He must go on. Again he Read outward, seeking that trace of cold fire, harder to find here amid the hot fire of stars, the cold ice of comets.

Just as he feared the trail was lost, he found it again, ashes of exhausted power. Again he put his "self" in its center, and shifted to another plane.

Winds howled and groaned. Astral forces ripped Torio from the "place" where he had entered, whipping his presence about helplessly, disorienting him.

In the moaning, weaving wind, though, he sensed again the expended power—somehow found the current that would take him to where it alone hung suspended in the center of the storm—and there he shifted planes again, into more wailing—

But these were people wailing! Spirits lost on the planes of existence—helpless, hopeless, gone mad with their inability to find their way either back to their bodies or onward to the plane of the dead!

//Melissa!// Torio projected, both hoping and fearing to find her here. //Melissa—come back with me! We need you, Melissa—*I* need you!//

He was answered by mocking howls. //Mellllisss-ssaaaa! Mellllisssaaa! Mellissaa!//

Incoherent beings surged around him, challenging his presence.

Minds grasped at his—twisted minds that echoed Maldek's power-madness. Minds that rejected death.

And out of the chaos one mind he knew—

Not Melissa!

Another mind, recognizing him, bent on destroying him as he had destroyed her—!

//Portia!// he identified. The corrupt Master of Masters who had died in the earthquake at Tiberium!

//Torio!// she challenged. //Lenardo's minion! You tried to kill me—but you killed only my body. I've been waiting for you—all of you, Lenardo, Aradia, Melissa—//

//Melissa? Is she here?// Torio interrupted, terrified that the evil woman had Melissa trapped in this place of madness.

//Yes!// she told him. //Melissa is mine, now. Come, Torio—enter our company if you wish to find her!//

But Portia no longer had the control of a Master Reader. Torio Read clearly her surprise at his question, and her spontaneous, opportunistic lie. In truth, she had not seen Melissa.

//You are lying,// he told her flatly—but he was unable to conceal his disappointment.

Portia answered him with angry laughter. //You've lost her, have you? Well, you've gained *me*, blind Torio! Still alive, aren't you? Stay here with me awhile—and then when I have properly trained you, I will send you back to do my work. I left far too much undone, thanks to you!//

As Torio remained conversing with Portia, the chaotic mass of garbled minds drifted out to surround him—would trap him here if he did not escape.

As they could not escape—

He dared not go in such a way as to show them how, to spread their madness throughout the planes of existence!

He was trapped here, as effectively as Portia!

But he had learned something about manipulating those who could Read thoughts—from Maldek, of all people.

//Yes, Portia,// he told her, //you did leave too much undone. Teach me how to wield power. I am searching for Melissa to learn both Reading and Adept powers. But you can teach me to rule better than she can. Show me, Portia—show me how you, a Reader confined to the Academy, gained power within the Aventine Empire next only to the Emperor's own!//

Her mental laughter was sarcastic this time. //He only *thought* my power was second to his,// she replied. //A few more years, and I would have ruled the empire, the Emperor merely my puppet. You wish to learn this, Torio? Yes, I knew you sought power when you fled the Academy. You will work well for me. Let me show you how I rose to power, that you may do the same.//

And her mind began to conjure up images of the past, of a royal child identified as a Reader, condemned—as she perceived it—to the poverty and powerlessness of the Academy, where she grew into the most powerful Reader within memory.

Not only Torio watched and listened; so did the others on this plane, drawn to the tale of manipu-

lation and extortion, gathering mentally about the
storyteller as Torio carefully edged his presence
away from Portia's self-absorption.

As he reached the edge of the circle of yearning
minds, though, Portia noticed that her audience
had shrunk by one.

//Torio—come back!// she projected—but she was
too late. Other minds shielded him from Portia.
His diversion had worked as effectively as Maldek's.

He shifted planes, and quickly shifted again, the
technique to guarantee privacy—or escape—even
if someone succeeded in pursuing him through
the first shift.

But he had lost all trace of the cold fire.

//Melissa!// he projected hopelessly. Her name
echoed back to him—he was on a finite plane, it
seemed. Yes, he could Read its dimensions as he
could not the others'. And, as with so many of the
planes of existence, his was the only presence here.

Wherever "here" was.

He could go on shifting planes endlessly—but
what good would that do? The chances of finding
the plane Melissa was on were too small to calculate.

He was lost.

Still . . . he could not give up.

He shifted planes, and found a world where he
was bombarded by tastes and smells instead of
sights and sounds.

Another shift, and music such as he had never
heard in the world he came from rang out in
absolute purity. He was held, spellbound. There
were no instruments or voices. It was pure music
itself—perhaps the plane from which musicians
like Zanos and Astra drew their inspiration? Or to

which they contributed the pure forms of their compositions?

If so, then ... artists also reached out to the planes of existence while in their bodies!

And most were not even Readers.

If an artist could tap this plane the way Maldek tapped the planes of power, then surely Torio could reach out to the plane on which Melissa was ...?

He envisioned her, then let her mental image rise in his mind, her sweet thoughts, her gentle caring, her strong will when she knew she was right—

Without knowing how, Torio suddenly discovered his "direction," shifted planes, and found Melissa.

She was with Dirdra, Kwinn, and Bryen.

They were visual—he could actually see Melissa's heart-shaped face and curling hair, Dirdra and Bryen's red locks—but both Bryen's hands were there and whole.

As for Kwinn—

He was a man, close to Dirdra's age, tall and strong and whole. The light of intelligence shone in the green eyes identical to his sister's.

Torio understood that the nonReaders could not comprehend their nonphysical selves except in the form they were accustomed to—but perfected.

And this plane was also a plain—land below, sky above, lighted even though no sun was visible. It took the form expected by those who traveled it.

Ahead on the plain was a huge stone archway, other travelers walking toward it from many directions. They might have burned or frozen to death in Madura's conflict, but here they were whole and healthy, hurrying eagerly toward that entryway into light.

That archway—or was it a tunnel?—was the source of the light illuminating this world.

Realizing that they perceived his usual appearance, Torio stood before his four friends, blocking their way.

"Torio," said Kwinn. "I know you—you are Dirdra's friend, and therefore mine."

"I am glad to meet you at last, Kwinn," Torio replied, "but I have come for Melissa."

"Torio," she replied mildly, "you do not belong here. It is not yet your time."

"Nor yours," he reminded her. "Come back with me, Melissa."

"I cannot," she told him. "I died. I belong on the plane of the dead."

"Maldek didn't die—but he will not recover without a healer. If there is no one with the power to restore his lands, your death is meaningless. Everyone in Madura will die, and the land will remain a frozen waste."

It was the right appeal, catalyzing Melissa's need to care for others. "But I must guide—" she began.

"We are here now," said Dirdra.

"We know the way," added Kwinn, taking his sister's hand.

"Tell Zanos," added Bryen, "that I am happy we found one another again."

Torio was rather surprised that the three showed no interest in returning to the world from which they had been so abruptly torn, but Melissa smiled at them. "We will remember you," she said, not offering to touch them—nor did Torio. He and

Melissa did not belong here . . . yet. Apparently
Dirdra and Kwinn and Bryen understood that
they did.

They Read when their appearance vanished to
the three nonReaders, although to one another
Torio and Melissa were as much "there" as ever.

But in a moment Melissa confessed, //Torio—I
do not know the way back.//

//I think I do,// he replied. //Not the way I came—
Portia will be lying in wait along that path.//

//Portia!//

//She is with those who refuse to accept death. I
made certain she could not follow me.//

//I hope so!// Melissa agreed. //How do we get
home?//

//Zanos and Astra are waiting, keeping your body
alive,// Torio told her. //I think I know of a plane
from which we can reach them. Come—//

Together, they moved from where they were,
to—

Cold white fire!

//No!// Melissa screamed mentally as it tried to
suck her back into its grasp.

In its own sphere, the white fire had utter purity, not evil here, where it belonged—merely
existence.

//Melissa—stop fighting it!// Torio urged—for
he recognized that just as Dirdra, Kwinn, and
Bryen had made images of themselves for coping
with a new plane of existence, Melissa had an
image of that power sucking energy from her,
trying to pull her in as it had done when it entered their world.

But here, it remained in balance so long as
there was no entry for it into another plane.

Melissa struggled, her own expectations causing the power to attack her.

//Melissa—observe!// Torio commanded—like a Master Reader instructing a pupil.

Melissa's Academy instinct took over. Her struggle subsided . . . and Torio showed her that out of body they could not feel cold—they had no physical energy for it to drain from them. Then he imagined the cold white fire drawing back from her, leaving her untouched, untainted.

//How—how did you do that?// she asked in awe.

//Read the power,// he replied. //It is in equilibrium here—it takes only a thought to manipulate it. Go ahead—you can do it as well as I.//

And Melissa discovered that she could.

Her relief, however, did not last long. //We are still lost,// she observed. //This is not where you meant to come, is it?//

//No, I meant to find the plane of music—but Melissa, there is also a direct path from this plane to our world. Through Maldek.//

//Through—?//

//How often did he tap this power? If we seek him from here—//

//What if we unleash this power into Madura again?//

//We won't. We know how to control it now.//

//We do?// she asked skeptically. //What happens once we return? You know how different things seem out of body.//

//I know,// he replied. //But Maldek controlled this power while in his own body—so can you. You will need it, Melissa. Your body died. Zanos and Astra are forcing your heart to beat, your

lungs to breathe—but there is great damage from
the cold. Probably to my body too, by now. You
will have much healing to do. Only by using this
power as Maldek did will you have the strength.//

She remained silent for some time, studying
the cold white fire surrounding them, so quiet
and harmless now. But open that circuit—

//Melissa,// Torio suddenly realized, //the secret
is never to allow the power to reach beyond your
own touch. Remember? Maldek sent it out to
attack Rokannia and the other sorcerers—that's
when he lost control.//

//But it is an evil power,// she insisted. //Why did
Madura turn so cold, long before we arrived? It
had to be this power Maldek was using—//

//Or simply his neglect of the climate,// Torio
speculated. //I've come to understand that power
isn't evil. Only what we do with it is good or evil.
You are good, Melissa. You will use this power
to heal—we've seen it used for that.//

He got the impression of a nod from her. //You
are right. So . . . let us try to go back before
Zanos and Astra become too tired to keep my
body alive any longer.//

Torio let the Master Sorcerer's image enter his
mind, Maldek's body lying as he had left him
with Cassandra, before the fire. Around him he
envisioned the ruined throne room, and his own
body and Melissa's side by side, Gray curled up
against his, Zanos and Astra sitting cross-legged,
concentrating on keeping Melissa alive—

He was cold!

Cold and weak as he had never been in his life!

In shock, Torio let his "self" drift upward
again, and found that he had been drawn to

Maldek's body, not his own, as he had been visualizing the throne room from that perspective.

All he had felt was the physical discomfort—Maldek was still unconscious, in body but without thought.

His own body drew Torio home; he settled in to the unwelcome weight and clumsiness that he always felt upon returning, this time accompanied by cold and numbness. Before he dared move, he Read his body's condition.

His fingers and toes were frozen, as were his ears and the tip of his nose. They would have to be warmed carefully, blood pumped through, healing fire sent—

Even as he thought it, not the heat of healing he had experienced so often, but the white fire of the plane of power tingled throughout his body, sliding into every cell, every nerve, restoring, then . . . warming? He didn't understand how cold could warm, but it happened even as he Read.

In moments, all was well—he was even comfortably warm, although the room was still unbearably cold. He sat up, opened his eyes—

And saw blurred light and hazy figures.

Torio blinked. When his eyes were closed, he Read the room perfectly, but when he opened them—

He was seeing!

Gray nudged him, and he absently patted the fuzzy gray blur.

"Torio—are you all right?" asked Zanos.

"Yes," he replied, closing his eyes to blank out the disturbing vision—he would worry about that later. At the moment—"Melissa?"

He Read her, back in her body but, like Maldek, unconscious.

"She'll be all right," said Astra. "She started breathing on her own a few moments ago, and her heart's beating. Read her, Torio—you succeeded. Melissa's *there*."

"Why didn't she heal her own body first?" he asked.

"What do you mean?" asked Zanos, and then Read Torio in his clumsy fashion. "I see—you've been healed already."

Torio was still Reading Melissa. "Why isn't she healing herself? I don't understand!"

"Torio, she's unconscious," said Astra. "There's other damage to her body besides freezing. Maldek hasn't gone naturally into healing sleep, either— they're too badly injured to do so without the aid of another healer."

"Then . . . who healed me?" he asked—opening his eyes when he turned to Astra, a polite gesture of ingrained habit, to appear to be seeing the person he spoke to.

But he *did* see Astra, blurrily in the flickering firelight. He frowned, and her image came clear. Then he understood: he had to learn to focus his eyes.

"It wasn't me," Astra answered his question. "It's been all Zanos and I could do to keep ourselves from freezing while we maintained Melissa's body."

"But . . ."

A frightening suspicion formed in Torio's mind.

He squatted down beside her and tentatively reached out to touch Melissa's forehead, envisioning her warm, her ravaged nerves soothed and healed, her cells restored—

The cold fire tingled through his fingertips and spread through Melissa's body, performing its work as speedily as before. Melissa opened her eyes, looked into his, and smiled.

Torio was so astonished that he rocked back on his heels and sat down on the cold stone floor, hard.

Zanos and Astra were staring at him in amazement. "You've finally learned—?" Zanos began.

"He's learned Maldek's technique!" said Astra. "Torio—"

"Yes—I *know* how dangerous it is," he replied. "Melissa—can you do it now?"

"Melissa's just been healed," said Zanos. "You can't expect her to have any strength until she's had a meal and a good long sleep."

"But I'm neither tired nor hungry," said Melissa, sitting up. "I'm just frightened of that power."

"You think I'm not?" asked Torio. "But if it means I can heal—"

"Yes," she said, and got gracefully to her feet. "I really do feel perfectly well," she reassured Zanos and Astra. "Torio—show me how to do that." And she knelt beside Cassandra.

"All I did was to envision you well," he replied.

But when Melissa tried it, she produced the usual heat of Adept healing, drawing on the energy of her own body as she had always done.

"You're still afraid of that power," said Torio. "It's only dangerous when misused. Think of the plane of power."

Tentatively, Melissa reached out—but could not tap the power. Yet she needed it—she was a healer

who would do only good with it. Torio put his
hands over hers, as Maldek had done before—and
the cold white fire spread outward through their
patient. In moments, Cassandra was sitting up,
warm and healthy.

"Now," said Zanos, "what are you going to do
about Maldek?"

Melissa stared at him. "You're not suggesting
that we let him die, are you?"

"He let *you* die," the gladiator countered. "Surely
Torio wouldn't think of—"

"Zanos," Torio said quietly, "would you have us
do nothing?"

"*Yes!* He was supposed to die, wasn't he? You're
the one who said it—"

"Unless someone died his death. Which Melissa
did. Now . . . it is Melissa's decision," Torio stated.
"Maldek owes her his life. She has the right to
give it back to him or not—and also the power."

"You say power is good or evil according to
what we do with it," Melissa reminded Torio. "It is
also according to what we *don't* do with it. Maldek
did evil when he refused to use his powers for
healing. I will not make his mistake. Help me,
Torio." And she knelt beside the Master Sorcerer.

When Maldek's eyes blinked open a few minutes later, he stared at Melissa in disbelief. "You?
Am I dead, too?" He sat up and looked around.

"No, you're not dead yet," said Zanos. "You just
ought to be."

Maldek frowned and climbed to his feet. "It's
cold in here."

"It is cold everywhere in Madura," Cassandra
told him. "Read what you have done to your land,
Maldek."

"I will restore it," he said, looking from one to another of the survivors. "Why did you revive me?" he asked suspiciously.

"Only because not to heal you would have been to let you die," replied Melissa.

"Fools!" he sneered. "Now I suppose you expect gratitude?"

"No," said Torio, "just a sign that you have learned something."

"That I must restore my land and heal my people? I agree. It was foolish to neglect my property. Now, though—what shall I do with you?" He glanced toward the corpses of Dirdra, Kwinn, and Bryen. "I see you allowed Dirdra to die. That is a waste—she amused me. But then you also amuse me, Melissa. You will take her place."

He held out his hand toward her, and became blank to Reading—but the power that he commanded merely tugged gently at Melissa. She resisted easily.

Maldek stared. "What have you done to me?" he demanded, bracing to use more force. Again it was not enough to make Melissa take a step in his direction.

"Answer me, woman!" he roared, lifting a huge hand as if to strike her. "How have you destroyed my powers?"

Torio stepped in front of Melissa. "You destroyed them yourself, Maldek," he replied, Reading deep into the core of the man's mind and body, discovering in his mental presence strange scarlike effects such as he had never Read before. "When you loosed that force through yourself," he interpreted, "you overloaded your abilities. Whether time will heal you, I cannot tell—only that because you refused to yield your life, the power burned in you much longer than it did in Melissa, and consequently did far more damage."

"This is nonsense!" said Maldek. "*Any* damage can be healed. You think to cripple me, but I can use ordinary healing on myself—it will simply take longer, and then I will have my revenge," he said, looking past Torio to Melissa.

It was obvious he was not Reading perfectly, either. "I am stronger than you, Melissa," he warned. "When I am well, you will be as helpless before me as Rokannia was—and you, too, will beg for my favors!"

"Rokannia defied you," Melissa replied. "So will everyone you cannot cow into submission. Maldek— why can't you learn from your experience?"

"I don't take lessons from people less powerful than I am!" he replied, and, shoving Torio aside, he stalked out of the throne room.

Melissa went to Torio. "Why did you let him do that?" she asked.

"I'm not used to thinking like an Adept," he told her. "Besides—what good would it do Maldek to know that I now have more power than he has? He'll find out soon enough."

Indeed, Maldek discovered it the next day, when he came out of healing sleep and found his guests hard at work in the City, restoring his people.

The sun was shining, and a warm breeze had begun to melt the ice left from the freezing night. Torio and Melissa had spent part of the night shifting the prevailing winds into a pattern that would bring them over warm ocean currents before they crossed the island. They would not keep to that pattern without constant vigilance, but there were surely Adepts with the power to control the weather in Maldek's land.

Torio was astonished at the uses of his new powers. He was not accustomed to being exhausted, like an Adept—but even Readers became tired after the loss of a night's sleep. Now Torio found that he could call upon that source of power to refresh his own body, and go on working.

Torio, Melissa, Zanos, Astra, and Cassandra were all at the City infirmary when Maldek made his appearance—but by that time Zanos and Astra had exhausted themselves, and were sound asleep on a pallet in one of the wards. Cassandra and Melissa set people who were already well to gathering food for those recovering.

Maldek strode in to the usual starts of fear from his people—but today they were followed by resentment he could not miss. Everyone had lost friends and family, and they knew that out in the countryside others were dying simply because the healers could not spread themselves far enough.

More people came to the infirmary every hour. Here, away from the center of the attack, some without powers had survived—but they were both burned and frozen, and the healers wore themselves out healing them. All those who worked regularly in the infirmary were by now in recovery sleep, and Torio worked alone. Even with the speed of healing via the cold fire, he fell farther and farther behind as wagonloads of injured were brought in.

Concentrating on a patient, Torio was only vaguely aware of Maldek entering the room where he was working. But when the sorcerer began to Read what he was doing, it was with such lack of

finesse that he was forced into recognizing Maldek—
who registered both shock and fury.

"You've stolen my powers!" the Master Sorcerer
accused.

Too busy to put up with trivia, Torio snapped, "If
you're awake and better, Maldek, use what powers
you have to heal some of these people, or get out
of here!"

But Maldek strode across the room to where
Torio was turning from one bed to the next and
grasped the Reader by the arm. "I am rested and
healed so far as I can manage alone. But you have
cut off the power—redirected it to yourself! Give
it back to me!"

"So you can loose it again, to do even more
damage?" Torio demanded. "If I *could* keep it
from you, I would—but I suppose you'll get it
back eventually" he added, Reading that some of
that peculiar "scarring" he had noticed before had
disappeared from Maldek's presence.

The Master Sorcerer dropped Torio's arm and
cocked his head to one side, his cold blue eyes
staring into the Reader's. "You," he stated flatly,
"can see me."

"Yes," Torio told him. "As you said, it is convenient. But you are not. If you're not going to be
useful, at least don't prevent me from healing
your people." And he turned to the next patient.

Maldek Read the woman's wounds, then the
line of patients outside—and more wagons approaching.

"My people," Maldek murmured. Then, "Torio—
there are no healers working but you."

"The others worked all night—every one of them
is exhausted."

"So are you," said the sorcerer, "but you don't know it. One of the effects of drawing power from outside your own body is that you don't realize how tired your *mind* is becoming. Beware the temptation not to sleep at all."

"Thank you for the advice," Torio replied acidly, "but I have Read more than thirty people die while waiting to be healed, simply because I could not work fast enough. You are disturbing my concentration, Maldek."

"I will help you," the Master Sorcerer replied, and turned to the patient who had just been brought in.

Using ordinary healing fire, Maldek cleansed the man's burns of infection and started them to healing; the patient was carried out in deep restorative sleep. The sorcerer rapidly took care of three more, but then—

"Torio—you have healed fifteen people while I have healed four, and your patients are able to get up and help others, while mine must sleep for hours or days, and then rebuild their strength before they will be good for anything."

The Reader stretched his muscles, relieving the tension of concentration. "That's still four people who won't die waiting for me," he replied. "I'm grateful for your help."

"You're—?" Maldek laughed sardonically. "Why are you giving me *your* help, you fool? You and your friends could have walked out last night, sailed away from Madura, and left me to my problems. You know the condition I'm in. What's left of my population would rise against me, exhaust my powers, and kill me—and then you could come back and claim this land as your own."

"Is that what you would have done?" Torio asked.

"Yes," the sorcerer replied, "that's what I would have done . . . before." Torio Read confusion in Maldek's mind. "Now—I don't know," he confessed. "Perhaps your ways are better. They were my father's ways, and Borru's. When I followed them for a few days, I found it pleasant to be greeted with hope instead of fear. Even now, it is welcome to Read the gratitude of those for whom I can do so little."

"Then you will regain your powers," said Torio.

". . . what?"

"It is what I was taught—and what the Adepts were taught in the savage lands. Abuse your powers, and you will lose them. Use them for good, and they will grow. Even though it sometimes seems to be untrue for a time, inevitably the debt must be paid."

"Then give me back my powers," said Maldek, "that I may do good."

"Maldek, I haven't stolen them," said Torio. "I can't just return them, like giving back a borrowed cloak!"

"No, for you will not lose what you have gained. But Read that line of injured people outside. Even the two of us can't heal them all before some die—but we can save *more*."

Even as Maldek spoke, Torio Read a young man far back in the line give up his weak grasp on life. Others hung on tenuously, infection eating at their wounds. Many were tossing in fever, some in convulsions.

"How do you think I can give you back your powers?" he asked.

"Direct the power through me, as I did with

Melissa. Put me in touch with it, and I will quickly have my strength back."

Torio stared. If it worked, would Maldek use his powers for good? Or was this a trick? The Master Sorcerer did want to heal—and if his motives were not purely selfless, how many people's motives were? Besides—his own powers were now equal to those Maldek had had. The man had to know that Torio could counter any sinister move.

The death in convulsions of a child out in the hallway tipped the scales.

"Very well," said Torio. "I will try."

Together they bent over the next patient. Maldek placed a hand on the forehead of a boy with a skull fracture from being hit by one of the giant hailstones. It had taken hours for what was left of his family to dig him out of the rubble of their home, and bring him here.

There was a huge blood clot in the boy's brain—it would be at least an hour's exhausting work for an Adept healer to dissolve the clot, move the bone back into place, and restore the damaged brain tissue. If it could be restored at all.

But with the cold fire, all was done in moments. Torio let it flow through his hand to Maldek's— and when he broke the contact, the flow continued. The Master Sorcerer had been right: once he was put back in touch with that source of power, he knew how to retain contact with it.

While the attendants removed the patient and brought in another, Maldek let the power flow through his own body, soothing the last of the "scarring" away.

By time time Torio was healing the other patient in the room—and the two men worked rapidly on, one burned and battered body after another, pausing only when the attendants brought them food and drink.

It seemed as if it would never end.

Zanos and Astra resumed work in another treatment room. In a third, the Maduran healers did so as well.

Cassandra administered medicines to the few patients whose injuries were so slight that herbs and simples were all they needed.

Melissa used Adept power to heal a number of people, and had to go sleep it off.

Torio was peripherally aware of all those events, but his main concentration remained on his patients.

Until at last the attendants took away the man he had just healed—and did not bring in anyone else.

It was a new morning; he had worked through a second straight night.

Pressing his hands to the small of his back, he stretched—and let the healing power ease his tension as he yawned.

Maldek turned from his last patient, and grinned. "No one can say the Lord of the Land didn't do his part this time!"

Torio restrained himself from reminding Maldek that it was his fault so many had died or been injured.

The healers and their assistants could take over the patients still in healing sleep. Everyone else had gone home, or to the shelters set up for those whose homes had been destroyed.

Torio and Maldek gathered Melissa, Zanos, Astra, and Cassandra, and returned to the castle. There the Master Sorcerer's surviving servants had been at work. Most of the debris of the battle had been cleared away, and a new kitchen set up. A meal was waiting for them in the dining hall.

There was not much conversation, for even those who had had some sleep were tired. Torio felt peculiar—not sleepy, yet not quite himself. A few hours of sleep would do him good.

But as they rose to go to their rooms, Maldek said, "Melissa, you come with me." And all could Read his intentions.

Melissa stared at him in disbelief. "Even if you loved me, which you don't," she said, "how could you be interested in making love after what we have just been through?"

"After a man has done something to be proud of? That is the very best time. Can you think Torio loves you, Melissa, when he does *not* want you now?"

Unfortunately, Melissa could Read only too easily that physical desire was the farthest thing from Torio's mind at that moment—but she only smiled at him and said, "I know Torio, and I love him. The fact that we feel exactly the same lack of desire at this moment only proves how much we are alike."

Maldek smiled in malicious delight. "But it is opposites who attract, Melissa. Come—let me show you what pleasures a Master Sorcerer can offer."

Torio found himself shaking his head, confused by what he was seeing, hearing, and Reading. What was Maldek trying to do? And why at this inappropriate moment?

Then he Read arousal in Melissa—the same thing Maldek had done to Dirdra in the memory they had all witnessed what now seemed a lifetime ago.

"Stop that!" Torio said, moving between Maldek and Melissa. Gray growled threateningly at Maldek, but was silenced by a thought from Torio.

"Do you want her?" Maldek asked.

"I love her," Torio replied.

"Will you fight me for her?"

"Fight? Why should I?"

"Because otherwise I am going to take her," Maldek said in tones that indicated that he found his outrageous statement perfectly reasonable.

And Torio found himself paralyzed as Maldek reached around him and took Melissa by the arm.

Torio called on his newfound powers, and broke free to grasp Melissa's other arm. "Let go, Maldek. I didn't restore your powers so you could hurt Melissa!"

"*You* restored his powers?!" demanded Zanos. "Torio—have you gone mad?"

"Perhaps," he replied. "At the time, there were dying people to be saved. But now—"

"Now you see how powers are to be used," said Maldek. "It's for good, Torio. I'm not going to hurt Melissa—you'll see. Just ask her tomorrow."

Melissa's physical desire was increasing—and then she stopped resisting as Maldek reached into her very mind.

"No!" cried Torio. "She's exhausted with healing. Melissa—fight him!"

But her lovely eyes stared at him as if he were the one being unreasonable.

Maldek draped Melissa's arm over his. "If you won't fight for her, Torio, you don't deserve her," he said, starting to lead her, unresisting, from the room.

"By Mawort!" exclaimed Zanos. "If you won't

fight him, Torio, I will! Can you call yourself a Reader and think she *wants* that beast?"

And Zanos picked up the carving knife from the table and flung it after Maldek.

Of course it did not connect; without even turning, the Master Sorcerer stopped it and let it clatter to the floor.

"Torio, *do* something!" pleaded Astra.

//Melissa!// he projected. //Break free, Melissa!//

And from somewhere deep within her mind, she answered, //Help me, Torio—oh, please—// And the thought broke off as Maldek found that part of her consciousness and turned it to desire for him as they started up the stairs toward the part of the castle where his room was—

Blessed gods! He is twisting her mind!

To his horror, Torio realized that he had actually doubted Melissa—

It was all Maldek's doing!

He ran to the door of the dining hall, stared at Maldek's retreating back—and willed a thunderbolt to strike him!

The crack shook the walls, and Maldek fell to his knees—only momentarily stunned, for he had been braced for an attack.

But it was enough to make him lose concentration on Melissa. She pulled free and ran down the stairs.

Maldek rose, laughing gleefuly, and turned to face Torio. "At last—the confrontation! Now my game comes to its final match!" And he flung lightning in his turn.

Some new instinct caused Torio to draw the cold fire into his body as protection—Maldek's bolt bounced off him harmlessly.

He leaped for the Master Sorcerer, tackling him
as Zanos had taught him, the two of them rolling
on the floor. He was peripherally aware of Zanos
holding Gray back, lest the dog join in the fray.

Maldek knew no ordinary defense for such an
attack—with his powers, why would he ever need
to learn it? So for a moment he was helpless with
surprise.

Practice against Zanos' huge size and strength
stood Torio well. The larger man reached for his
throat, and the Reader flipped him backward, to
land with a breathtaking crash.

But Maldek was no street brawler. Even as he
drew a burning breath into his lungs, he set Torio's
shirt afire.

That was nothing, out in an instant.

But the instant was long enough for Maldek to
recover—and this time when he reached for Torio
his hands sent currents of *pain* through the Reader!

"Give it up, Torio," said Maldek. "The woman
is mine!"

"No!" Torio gasped, struggling to break free.
"Melissa is mine—you have no right to her!"

He remembered his powers once again, and
drove the pain backward into Maldek, conjuring
the searing of cold fire into the sorcerer's nerves
as he tried to burn him out, put him back to what
he had been, helpless to force Melissa—

"Torio! *Torio!*"

It was Melissa's horrified voice that broke his
concentration, her cool hands that touched his,
breaking him free from Maldek and taking the
cold fire into herself.

Only then did he realize that his hands had
been about Maldek's throat, choking the life from

him. He felt her disbelief at what he had done—
and sank into self-loathing as he realized that he
had been brawling mindlessly over the woman he
loved, as if she were a piece of property. Shame
burned his face.

But Maldek grasped his opportunity. Melissa
was touching him. Torio was too distracted to
oppose him.

The Master Sorcerer grasped Melissa's wrists
and pulled her to him, reaching out to take over
her mind again, drawing her face to his for a
kiss—

From Melissa, the white fire burned through
him for just one moment, shocking him into dropping her hands, staring at her—

As she stared back in shock. Then she looked
down at her hands, concentrated, and Torio Read
the cold fire flow through her, too—as it should
have been at her command ever since they had
visited the plane of power.

Maldek, Melissa, and Torio all climbed to their
feet. Maldek reached toward Melissa again, but
she looked up into his eyes and said coldly, "Do
not touch me."

Then she turned to the Reader. "And you,
Torio—I thought you loved me. But Maldek
brought out your true feelings—exactly the same
as his. Conquest! Proof of power! All you want is
to possess me!"

There was no hiding Torio's shame in the feelings Maldek had brought out of his subconscious.
For that moment he had, indeed, wanted Melissa
not for herself but as the prize he battled for.

When he could not reply, Melissa turned and

fled down the hall to the stairs leading to her own room.

One by one, the others followed, going silently to their own chambers, leaving Maldek standing alone, knowing that there were now two people capable of countering his powers.

"But why won't you stay?" Melissa asked Torio a few days later.

"Why *will* you?" he demanded in return. "Melissa, I'm so ashamed—my abuse of power caused you pain, but at least this time no one died."

"No—*I* am ashamed," she replied. "Maldek tricked us both. You had not slept for two days. Of course he was able to bring out your darker instincts. I should have known what he was doing."

"So should I," said Torio, "with Maldek as an example of how unlimited power releases those instincts! I didn't know such feelings were in me, Melissa. I cannot ever trust myself again until I learn how to control under every possible stress.

"Come with me—there must be other lands where people have both Reading and Adept powers, and use them without doing harm. They must have ways of training people to use power responsibly, as the Academies do for Reading."

Melissa sighed. "Torio, I am a healer, and there is a whole land here in need of healing."

"Maldek—"

"—is never going to change," she replied. "Anyone can see that. The only thing that will keep him from destroying his land altogether is a counterbalance—someone with powers equal to his."

"You," he was forced to admit. "You saved his

life, Melissa—and now you are responsible for him."

"Yes," she agreed. "When I realized that, I was able to tap the power. So you understand why I cannot go with you?"

He could not deny that he understood—but neither could he deny the imperative he felt more strongly with every passing day—a call from somewhere far to the east, lands no one he had ever met had visited.

He had spoken the words that brought Melissa here, to her destiny. Now he had to face the fact that his lay elsewhere. "It is as Maldek said—I found what I didn't know I was looking for: a direction for my life. But I don't know what lies in that direction."

"Will you come back?" Melissa asked.

"I . . . I cannot answer that," he said truthfully. "If I can return, Melissa, I will."

"I love you," she said softly. "I wish . . ."

"I do, too," he replied, "but the time is not right for us to be together. I love you, Melissa—but only the gods know whether we will ever meet again. If we do, we will be different people, for we both have much to discover about life, and about ourselves."

Melissa was not the only one of their party to stay behind; Astra's mother, Cassandra, would not return to the Savage Empire with her daughter. "Even my poor powers are needed here," she explained. "This was once the happiest home I ever knew. Now I have the chance to make it happy again."

But Zanos and Astra had obligations to the Savage Alliance, to Lilith in particular, and so they

perforce must leave once Madura showed signs
that it would recover from the havoc of the battle
of the sorcerers.

Torio sailed with them down the river to the
sea, between banks beginning to show the first
signs of green in recovery from the devastation.
The sun shone, and once clouds came up and
produced a warm shower. Maldek's land would
flourish under Melissa's care—and Torio knew
she had the strength to keep the Master Sorcerer
in line.

They sailed across the narrow channel, and put
Torio ashore just south of Brettonia. Not knowing
where he was going, he found his feet instinctively
taking the path while his newly opened eyes fas-
tened on the horizon. Carrying only a small bun-
dle of necessities, Gray trotting happily at his heels,
he turned toward the east in search of his own
destiny.

About the Author

Jean Lorrah is the creator of the *Savage Empire* series, in which *Sorcerers of the Frozen Isles* is the fifth book. The first four are *Savage Empire, Dragon Lord of the Savage Empire, Captives of the Savage Empire*, and *Flight to the Savage Empire* (the last one coauthored with Winston A. Howlett, and also available in a Signet edition). She is coauthor with Jacqueline Lichtenberg of *First Channel* and *Channel's Destiny* in Jacqueline's Sime/Gen series, and has written a solo novel in that series, *Ambrov Keon*. She is also the author of the professional *Star Trek* novel *The Vulcan Academy Murders*, and coeditor with Lois Wickstrom of *Pandora*, a small-press sf magazine.

Jean has a Ph.D. in Medieval British Literature, and is Professor of English at Murray State University in Kentucky. Her first professional publications were nonfiction; her fiction appeared in fanzines for years before her first professional novel was published in 1980. She maintains a close relationship with sf fandom, appearing at conventions and engaging in as much fannish activity as time will allow. On occasion, she has the opportunity to combine her two loves of teaching and writing by teaching creative writing.